"Don't leave me yet," he implored.

His mouth was too close to hers. Gabi felt the warmth from his body as his hands slid around her back and pulled her into him. "It's been too long since we last kissed each other. I have to kiss you again. I need to kiss you, if only for old time's sake."

"Jeff—" she cried helplessly as his dark head descended and his mouth covered hers in the old familiar way. Fourteen years might have passed, but still, her body seemed to know by instinct where to fit as she melted into him.

But the years had brought changes. He was kissing her with a man's kiss now, hot with desire and an urgency that caused her to forget time and place.

Dear Reader,

Saying goodbye to the Yosemite Ranger series is like saying goodbye to a dear friend you might not see again for years. Would it surprise you readers to learn that these rangers and wives along with their children and animals gave me hours and hours of writing enjoyment as I wrote their individual stories? If you've never had the opportunity to visit Yosemite National Park with its incredible abundance of flora and fauna, I hope one day you'll find a way to do so. Enjoy!

Rebecca Winters

"Don't leave me yet," he implored.

His mouth was too close to hers. Gabi felt the warmth from his body as his hands slid around her back and pulled her into him. "It's been too long since we last kissed each other. I have to kiss you again. I need to kiss you, if only for old time's sake."

"Jeff—" she cried helplessly as his dark head descended and his mouth covered hers in the old familiar way. Fourteen years might have passed, but still, her body seemed to know by instinct where to fit as she melted into him.

But the years had brought changes. He was kissing her with a man's kiss now, hot with desire and an urgency that caused her to forget time and place.

WITHDRAWN

Dear Reader,

Saying goodbye to the Yosemite Ranger series is like saying goodbye to a dear friend you might not see again for years. Would it surprise you readers to learn that these rangers and wives along with their children and animals gave me hours and hours of writing enjoyment as I wrote their individual stories? If you've never had the opportunity to visit Yosemite National Park with its incredible abundance of flora and fauna, I hope one day you'll find a way to do so. Enjoy!

Rebecca Winters

ABOUT THE AUTHOR

Rebecca Winters, whose family of four children has now swelled to include five beautiful grandchildren, lives in Salt Lake City, Utah, in the land of the Rocky Mountains. With canyons and high alpine meadows full of wildflowers, she never runs out of places to explore. They, plus her favorite vacation spots in Europe, often end up as backgrounds for her romance novels, because writing is her passion, along with her family and church. Rebecca loves to hear from readers. If you wish to email her, please visit her website at www.cleanromances.com.

Books by Rebecca Winters

HARLEQUIN AMERICAN ROMANCE

1261—THE CHIEF RANGER
1275—THE RANGER'S SECRET
1302— A MOTHER'S WEDDING DAY
      "A Mother's Secret"
1310—WALKER: THE RODEO LEGEND
1331—SANTA IN A STETSON
1339—THE BACHELOR RANGER

HARLEQUIN SUPERROMANCE

1034—BENEATH A TEXAS SKY
1065—SHE'S MY MOM
1112—ANOTHER MAN'S WIFE
1133—HOME TO COPPER MOUNTAIN
1210—WOMAN IN HIDING
1233—TO BE A MOTHER
1259—SOMEBODY'S DAUGHTER
1282—THE DAUGHTER'S RETURN

HARLEQUIN ROMANCE

4148—CINDERELLA ON HIS DOORSTEP
4172—MIRACLE FOR THE GIRL NEXT DOOR
4185—DOORSTEP TWINS
4191—ACCIDENTALLY PREGNANT!
4219—THE NANNY AND THE CEO

I would like to dedicate *Ranger Daddy* to the
small army of rangers and forest service workers
whose whole purpose is to help preserve
one of nature's glorious creations and
keep it safe for generations to come.

Chapter One

"Mrs. Rafferty? After what you told me in your phone message last evening, if you were my daughter I'd advise you, *unofficially,* to pack a bag and get to a safe place fast. Don't tell anyone where you are. Trust no one. If you tell anyone your location, you're exposing them to danger, too."

"I understand. How long do I need to be away?"

"I'll know better when I've talked to your ex-husband's attorney. After I find out what's going on, I'll call you back. But be prepared to be gone a week."

Gabi groaned. She would have to dip into her savings. And in three weeks she was due back at her elementary school in Rosemead, California, getting her classroom ready.

"Whatever you do, don't go home for any reason."

"I won't." Fear had caused Gabi's mouth to go dry, making it difficult to form the words.

"Good. We'll both keep in touch."

"Thank you for returning my call on a Saturday, Mr. Steel." Her voice shook.

"I know how anxious you are. Be careful."

"I will." She hung up and rushed around the little

guest cottage on the strand in Oceanside, California, packing things in her suitcase as fast as she could. Too bad she couldn't stay here longer, but the place was booked up a year in advance and the vacation she'd been planning since last fall was over. New guests would be moving in by three in the afternoon.

After grabbing some clothes and shoes for Ashley, she rushed into the living room, where her seven-year-old was watching morning cartoons. They hadn't eaten breakfast yet. Her precious daughter was still in her jammies.

"Honey?" Gabi picked up the remote from the arm of the couch and turned off the TV.

"How come you did that?" Ashley looked up in surprise.

"Because I decided we'll take that other little trip I promised you before school starts. Hurry and get dressed."

"But I thought we didn't have to check out of here until lunch. I want to play on the beach with those kids next door."

"I know you do, but we're going someplace else really neat and I want us to get an early start. It's the weekend, and the freeways will be crowded."

"What's it called?" Ashley asked as she put on her denims and save-the-whales pink top.

"Yosemite National Park." The answer had come to Gabi a split second after she'd hung up the phone. At least there she'd be well away from home while she got her head together and waited for Mr. Steel's next call. She would find the cheapest lodgings available to make their money stretch.

"Will it take a long time to get there?"

"Part of a day in the car, but you've got your portable DVD player and your favorite CDs. Don't forget Mr. Charles. I think he's behind the pillow on the bed." Ashley never went anywhere without her stuffed beagle. It was so old you couldn't tell the dog's breed anymore. "We'll stop for breakfast on the way. Okay?"

"Can I have sausage?"

"Yes." Anything to make Ashley happy on this stressful day.

After one more inspection to be certain she hadn't overlooked anything, Gabi dashed back to the bedroom to put on jeans and a T-shirt that matched Ashley's. They'd bought them at Sea World after seeing the show a few days earlier. Once she'd slipped on her sneakers, she packed all the toiletries in the bathroom, and they were ready.

The room had been paid for ahead of time. Gabi left the cottage key on the side table and they went out to her Honda Civic, parked in one of the tiny garages off the courtyard away from the beach. Ashley climbed in back with her things and fastened her seat belt. Gabi put their suitcases in the trunk and they headed to a nearby drive-through for breakfast.

After they'd eaten, she stopped at an ATM a few blocks away, then gassed up at the Mini Mart around the corner from the Coast Highway. While she waited for the tank to fill, she reached in her purse for her hairbrush and tried to make herself a little more presentable. She and her daughter both had short, curly dark hair, which, when rumpled, looked adorable on Ashley, but messy on her.

Soon they were on their way. Fortunately, the heaviest traffic was going the other way, to the beach cities. Before long they were headed north toward Fresno via Bakersfield. As the car ate up the miles, Gabi hoped the painful thudding of her heart would subside. But the phone call from her former foster mother, Bev White, now a widow but still living in Alhambra, California, had thrown her into a state of panic.

Your ex-husband is looking for you. He said he's back from his military service for good and wants to see his child. He left his phone number and address with me. When I reminded him he'd given up his parental rights, he told me his attorney would see about that.

Gabi was in shock. She was also outraged that he'd involved Bev. The woman who'd given Gabi foster care from the time she'd turned fourteen until she was eighteen still fostered other children. She shouldn't have to be involved in Gabi's problems at this stage in life. After Mr. Steel's warning, Gabi knew she couldn't tell Bev where she was going.

Gabi couldn't comprehend why Ryan suddenly wanted to see Ashley after all this time. He'd willingly given up all claim to their child, without even knowing the gender of the baby.

Gabi had met Ryan in Los Angeles at a wedding. She'd worked evenings for a catering service to help put herself through college. He was back from basic training in the Army, joining a unit that wouldn't be deployed to Japan for another year.

After she graduated from California State University, they got married and moved to San Marino, where he had an apartment. Their marriage, so promising in the beginning, had broken down fast when, ten months later, she told him she was pregnant. They'd used precautions, agreeing not to start a family for a couple years, but it had happened anyway.

Like turning on a dime, he'd suddenly presented a dark side she didn't understand.

We can fix that in a hurry. You're going to get an abortion. I don't want us going to Japan with a baby.

While Gabi stood there horrified, he'd said he'd changed his mind about ever wanting a family, that she was all he needed. Then he'd refused to talk about it.

He knew Gabi's feelings on the subject. Having been placed in five foster homes in her life, she would never end her pregnancy! What if her birth mother had made that decision? Gabi's mother had abandoned her at a train station when she was a newborn. Though she never knew her parents, they'd given her life!

But Gabi couldn't move Ryan. When she'd told him she wanted the baby more than anything in the world, he'd pushed her against the wall, bruising the back of her head.

I don't want this baby. Understand?

She'd thought he was going to do something worse. Like a blood-pressure band, his hands had tightened on her arms before he'd shoved her away.

Remember what I said. Let's get this pregnancy terminated.

Gabi had lived around other foster kids who'd come from homes filled with domestic violence. She'd learned early that if you didn't want to be violated, you didn't tolerate any abuse. When Ryan had hurt her and demanded she abort their baby, any love for him died on the spot, never to be resurrected.

Desperate for help, she'd left their apartment and driven to Bev's. The older woman told her to go straight to the YWCA and get into a shelter.

Gabi followed her advice. Once they took her in, the staff helped her find Mr. Steel, a divorce attorney in Los Angeles who was willing to work out the cost of his services in manageable payments. While Gabi stayed at the shelter, the attorney had her husband served with divorce papers, forcing him to find his own attorney.

In a surprise move, Ryan's attorney went for a plea bargain. Ryan would sign away his parental rights and agree to the divorce if Gabi refrained from pressing charges of abuse, so there'd be no chance of it showing up on his military record. He planned to make the Army his career.

That was fine with Gabi. She let him take more belongings from their apartment than was fair, so he'd have nothing to hold over her. In her naïveté she'd assumed that with the divorce decree granted, she would never have to see him or deal with him again.

"NOW YOU WILL FEEL NO rain, for each of you will be shelter to the other. Now you will feel no cold, for each of you will be warmth to the other. Now you will feel no more loneliness, for each of you will be a constant companion to the other."

With those words, Chief Sam Dick, the old, venerable Paiute chief of Yosemite, dressed in ceremonial garb, brought the wedding ceremony to a close. He nodded to the married couple, who turned to each other, their faces glowing with ineffable joy before they embraced.

To Ranger Jeff Thompson, chief steward of resources for Yosemite National Park, the sight of his best friend claiming the woman he'd loved for so long brought a lump to his throat. And a stab of envy.

The wedding blessing summed up what marriage was truly meant to be. But for circumstances beyond his control, Jeff knew he and the girl who'd stolen his heart years ago would have had that kind of union.

Ninety-nine percent of the time, he tried not to think about it. At this morning's ceremony, however, he'd been forced to relive his past, bringing back the ache that was never far from the surface. The only terror he'd ever known was at the possibility that he'd go to his grave never finding that kind of joy again.

After taking some pictures, he looked up at the giant sequoia trees forming the open-air cathedral. Their tops grazed the brilliant blue sky where an August sun blazed. Shafts of light found their way to the forest floor, gilding the small crowd gathered, and setting the silvery-gold hair of the bride on fire.

Alex Harcourt, exquisite in a simple white wedding dress that fell to her knees, was now the wife of Ranger Calvin Hollis. He stood tall in his uniform. Besides family and colleagues, the guests included the Zuni teenagers from New Mexico she'd brought to the park as volunteers. The scene was surreal, enchanted.

While everyone congregated around the ecstatic couple, Jeff slipped away, having celebrated with them the night before. Right now he was on duty and had to drive back to headquarters in Yosemite Valley.

As he climbed into the cab of his government-issue truck, Cal's black-and-white Karelian bear dog barked a greeting. "Hey, Sergei." Jeff gave him a rub behind the ears. "It's official. You're a family of three now. But for the next ten days, you're stuck with me." He started the engine and they took off.

Cal and Alex were starting out their life together by taking the teenagers back to their homes in Albuquerque. After a few days on her parents' ranch, they were flying to the Caribbean to enjoy a honeymoon. On their way back to the park they'd be stopping in Cincinnati to visit Cal's family.

It was a lot to pack in, but Jeff had never seen his friend happier. After their troubled history, if two people ever deserved some time off together, they did.

A little while later Jeff attached Sergei's leash and they entered the rear door of headquarters. Jeff popped his head inside his secretary's office. "I'm back, Diane."

"Hey! How was the wedding?"

"Out of this world. I'll show you the pictures later. With Chief Sam Dick presiding over the ceremony against those ancient trees, and Alex looking like— well, like only she can—there was a real spiritual feeling, you know? It gave me gooseflesh."

Again he found himself craving the same thing, but there was no chance of it happening to him again. One per customer in this life, if you were lucky.

"Now you've got the hairs standing on the back of my neck."

He smiled. His African-American assistant—a wife and mother—was one of the park's secret treasures.

Maintaining the human infrastructure that supported all the services provided within Yosemite Park was a Herculean task. Jeff couldn't do his job without her.

"Has Bryce arrived for the meeting yet?" Bryce Knolls was the chief construction engineer Jeff relied on to oversee big projects.

"He and the others you requested are in the conference room. At the moment they're enjoying doughnuts and coffee."

"You're a saint. I'll get my stuff together and join them." He walked into his office and reached for the files he'd been working on. Juggling the costs of maintenance to stay within the park's budget was a continual nightmare. When he'd been promoted from district ranger to chief steward of resources in May, it had come as a mixed blessing. More money, but more headaches.

"Come on, Sergei. I'm afraid you're in for a boring session, but I'll take you for a run this afternoon after my meeting."

The obedient dog trotted alongside him, alert. Last month Sergei had become famous nationwide for his help in cracking the worst bear-mutilation case in the park's history. Since he and Cal, along with two of Alex's teens who'd helped in the criminals' arrests, had been on TV, many tourists passing through the entrances to the park wanted to see Sergei and take pictures of him. One of the rangers jokingly commented he was as popular as Yosemite Falls.

Jeff chuckled. Poor Cal was besieged everywhere he went with his dog. But as his friend reminded him last night, the laugh was going to be on Jeff, who'd also been in the news. Since his department included overseeing the youth volunteer program for the park, the superintendent, Bill Telford, had given permission for the TV crew to film Jeff with Alex and all her volunteers.

"Gentlemen?" He entered the conference room, where a dozen men had gathered. "Excuse me for being a few minutes late." He put his materials on the table. "I just got back from attending Ranger Hollis's wedding at Mariposa Grove."

Bryce's black brows went up. "That's one fortunate man." Ex-senator Harcourt's gorgeous daughter had made her mark at the park in more ways than one.

"I think we can all agree on that." Jeff smiled. "Since I don't want to waste your time, let's get down to business. We've got some projects to take care of right away. There's a job that includes shoring up the south elevation of the Ranger's Club. It was done over ten years ago, but needs work again. So does the footbridge at Vernal Falls.

"I've also been out inspecting the damage from the frazil ice last April. The runoff from both Upper and Lower Yosemite Falls was so excessive, it wiped out several important footbridges on Yosemite Creek. Now that I've worked out the costs, they need to be rebuilt.

"Bryce? Here are the blueprints the architect put on my desk. I've added the specs. Diane made copies for everyone. It would have been nice to get them rebuilt in June, but there were other priorities. Take a look at everything. Ask me anything you want."

Marty lifted his head. "Before we get started, I have to ask if it's true that there's going to be a cap on the number of visitors to the park from now on?"

The other engineer's question was off the subject, but Jeff was happy to answer it because there'd been a lot of talk lately about changes coming. "As you know, everyone and his dog has been trying to figure out the overall carrying capacity of Yosemite Valley. No pun intended in reference to Ranger Hollis or Sergei."

The men chuckled.

"To be specific, no one has the answer to that yet, so no, there's no cap. That should settle rumors that we're closing off areas to the public, as some have assumed. But since the Merced River, for instance, is an incredibly valuable resource, we want to make sure it's protected. Therefore, the new building projects for that area are being put off until next year."

His explanation generated talk for a few minutes. "Does that include a moratorium on the restoration of facilities at Curry Village?" Bryce finally asked.

"Looks like it," Jeff answered. "There were plans to move the endangered cabins out to the parking-lot area, away from the cliff, but Chief Rossiter hasn't been given the final okay on that yet. There are a hundred million dollars' worth of projects for the park still being kept on hold. While the experts worry about Yosemite's fragile ecosystem and how best to preserve it, we'll concentrate our efforts on repairing historic buildings, damaged trails and the like."

"Is there any truth to the rumor that some of the housing is going to be permanently removed from the valley? Several politicians are claiming that existing structures aren't the best thing for the environment. I'm afraid the sentiment is catching on," Marty stated.

"That subject has been floated around by environmentalists for years, but the answer is no, and in my opinion always will be no."

"That's good," the engineer said. "My wife and I were talking about it this morning. Neither of us relishes the thought of having to live outside the park and commute."

"None of us do. It would be unwise to remove and relocate housing for the sake of reducing beds. Our visitors require service, and moving employees out of the valley means increasing transportation. All it will do is impact our roads and pollute our air."

"Amen," Bryce exclaimed. "It would make it damn hard to hire the highly qualified personnel we need, let alone retain them."

Jeff nodded. "Living in Yosemite Valley is an important incentive to many people like you and me, who prefer life away from the big city. And it allows us who have close contact with the tourists to be that much more familiar and knowledgeable about the valley and the park itself."

He looked around, but there didn't seem to be any more questions. "All right. Go ahead and read through everything. If something's not clear, we'll talk about it."

While they got busy, Jeff took a doggy treat out of his pocket and leaned down to feed it to Sergei. "Hey, buddy," he whispered. "I need to check out North Pines Campground while you sniff for bears. How's about we do that after I'm through here?" He was glad for the dog's company.

At the thought of Cal leaving for his honeymoon, Jeff realized he had to do something about his love life. To wallow in pain for the rest of his days wasn't healthy. A psychiatrist would probably tell him he was in a depression, and needed to shake it. But how was he supposed to do that when he was still waiting to experience the intense kinds of feelings he'd had for a certain female back in high school?

Her foster mother hadn't liked it that Jeff lived next door. Neither had Jeff's father. In collusion with his second wife, Ellen, he'd made sure the relationship was broken up before anything happened that couldn't be undone, such as pregnancy. Jeff had been forced to leave Alhambra at eighteen, and that was it.

In his second year of college he'd tried to bury his pain by getting married, but it was a disaster, and had ended in divorce by the beginning of his third year. Somewhere in his psyche he'd known it was destined to fail. Though the divorce hadn't put him off women, so far he couldn't see himself making a permanent commitment a second time, not if he wasn't deeply in love.

After he'd told Cal about his past, his friend no longer questioned why his relationships with women never went anywhere. Of course they didn't, when Jeff was unconsciously searching for what he'd once known in his youth and had never found again. That kind of love truly was wasted on the young.

Since being transferred to Yosemite, Jeff mostly dated women outside the park. He didn't like the idea of getting involved with another ranger. When he went off duty for twenty-four hours, he wanted a total change, and usually took off on his motorcycle.

In fact, he was going to do his yearly charity stunt

ride in North Fork next Saturday, to benefit the fund for children of fallen firefighters in the area. If Denise Anderson was available, he'd take her out to dinner afterward. The attractive woman, who worked for their chamber of commerce, had caught his eye.

He ought to phone her to make sure she'd be free, but he couldn't seem to muster the enthusiasm right now. Maybe tonight. That's what was wrong with him. The world abounded in good-looking women, but not one ignited him.

He grimaced when he realized Cal's marriage had made him morose and restless. For the time being, Sergei was welcome to run him ragged.

AT THE ENTRANCE to Yosemite, a ranger told Gabi she might have trouble finding a vacancy for the night in Yosemite Valley. "You could get lucky if there's a sudden cancellation, but without reservations you never know if you'll find a place to stay. August is high season and the summer crowds reduce your chances of success. I'd advise you to make one outside the park for tonight as a precaution."

He gave her a list of possible locations close by. After three phone calls, she was able to find a room for her and Ashley. "Thanks for your help, Ranger Ness." His name tag was pinned to his uniform. "The Travelodge in El Portal has a space for us tonight."

"Good. Enjoy your visit to Yosemite, ma'am." The ranger smiled at Gabi with male interest as he tipped his hat.

"I'm sure we will."

With the fee paid and Ashley poring over the park

literature, Gabi passed through the South Entrance, experiencing a feeling of safety. It was ridiculous, but the act of entering the park made her feel as if an invisible door had closed behind them, protecting them from danger.

She'd never been here before, but had hoped to come one day. Her stomach muscles clenched. *Just not under these circumstances.*

"Look, Mom!"

"I can't right now, honey. What does the brochure say?"

"There's a train we can ride. It's called the Yo-sem-ite Moun-tain Sugar Pine Rail-road."

Her daughter had been the top reader in her first-grade class last year and it showed.

Her darling girl, whom Ryan hadn't wanted any part of.

Gabi tightened her hands on the steering wheel, aware she was running on sheer adrenaline. Her ex-husband had shown an unpredictable side to him years ago. It appeared time hadn't changed him. She shuddered to think his violent nature hadn't changed, either, not if he'd gone straight to Bev's, demanding to know where Gabi was.

"That sounds fun. We'll go exploring later." The ranger had suggested she could still try to get a room at Yosemite Lodge. There were other possibilities, too, such as the canvas tent cabins at Curry Village in Yosemite Village, where the park headquarters were located.

Gabi had decided that if she ran into trouble finding accommodations for the rest of the week, someone at the desk would know where she could locate Jeff Thompson, the striking ranger whose picture had been in the newspaper last month.

The last time she'd seen him had been on a Friday evening fourteen years ago, when he'd brought her home from a movie on his motorcycle. He'd told her he had special plans for them that weekend, but they'd never materialized. After kissing her until she could hardly breathe, he'd said good-night, and she'd run into Bev's house, not realizing she wouldn't be seeing Jeff again.

A lot of years had gone by since then, but at one time they'd been very close. If she could find him, maybe he would know of a place they could stay inside Yosemite.

In the news photo, he'd been standing next to the beautiful daughter of a former senator from New Mexico. They'd cracked a bear-mutilation case along with another ranger and his dog, also featured in the news. Since reading the story, Gabi hadn't been able to get the image of a very grown-up Jeff out of her mind.

"Here's a picture of people horseback riding." Ashley broke into her thoughts. "It says 'Children must be at least seven years old to ride.' That means *I* can go. 'You can ride to the top of a wa-ter-fall.' You should see how tall it is, Mom! I want to do that. Can we?"

"Maybe," she answered absently, too frightened by what had happened in the past eighteen hours to concentrate.

Gabi had told Ashley as much as she felt her daughter could handle about her father. She'd explained that their marriage hadn't worked out and they'd divorced. Her father had gone overseas in the military long before she'd been born, and had never been back.

Ashley had accepted that explanation. Of course, the time would come when she'd want to know more, but Gabi hadn't anticipated a discussion like that for a while longer. Fresh spurts of panic attacked her every time she thought about Bev's phone call last evening.

Tanned and happy, Gabi had just come in from a walk in the surf with Ashley when her cell phone buzzed. Bev's news had devastated her on the spot. She tensed now, anxious to get to their destination, but the traffic was moving at turtle speed. At this rate it would take forever to get there. Gabi had the sinking feeling every possible place to sleep in Yosemite Valley would be filled, and was grateful for the ranger's advice to have an alternate plan.

Thank goodness Ashley had forgotten how tired she was. At the moment she was entertaining herself looking at the brochures and reading about the various granite formations and animals.

"It says there are three hundred to five hundred black bears in the park. I can't wait to see one!"

"Me, neither," Gabi murmured automatically, her grim thoughts elsewhere as they rounded a curve.

"Mom!" her daughter suddenly blurted. "Look!"

Gabi gasped, catching sight of a famous landmark in the distance. For a moment she forgot the frightening reason why she'd fled here. The wonderful view literally took her breath away. "It's fantastic!"

"But in this picture there's a waterfall. Where is it?"

"I didn't realize it would be this dry, but it *is* August." Drivers in the other cars were probably thinking the same thing. But in response to the beauty around them they'd reduced their speed to ten miles an hour. She had no choice but to keep following the cars in front of her, but she was growing impatient.

Eventually they came to the heart of the valley, and Gabi found a spot near Curry Village where they could park. "Come on, honey. Let's get out and stretch our legs." With a lot of luck, maybe there'd be a cancellation and they could find a cabin right here for tonight, instead of having to leave the park.

A half hour and several phone calls later, she had to give up. "Every hotel and lodging area is full for the weekend. It's my fault because I didn't phone ahead." Gabi had been too frantic to think.

"Does that mean we have to go back to that other place now?" Ashley's eyes had filled with tears. She was hungry and tired after their drive from the beach.

"Yes, honey, but we'll get some tacos over there first. Okay?" She hugged her. "That ranger I talked to told me the Travelodge has a pool, and it won't take us long to get there." Ashley loved to swim. "Come on. I'm hungry, too." Gabi took her hand. Maybe they'd just stay at El Portal and take day trips into the park until she knew what her next move would be.

Gabi had intended to walk over to headquarters to ask if Jeff Thompson was around, but at the last minute she changed her mind. In fact, she'd gotten cold feet about the whole idea. What did you say to someone you hadn't seen in years?

Hi, Jeff! I'm running away from my ex. I used to

talk to you about everything. Could you help me find a room for tonight?

How lame and pathetic and desperate sounding was that for a supposedly stable thirty-one-year-old woman? When she thought about it, her behavior wasn't that different from that of Ryan, who'd shown up after almost an eight years' absence, unwanted and uninvited.

It's off-the-wall desperate, Gabi.

She was ashamed to realize how close she'd come to doing something completely ludicrous. Today she'd been out of her mind. After a good night's sleep she'd be able to think better, without needing help from anyone else.

When Mr. Steel had told her to find a safe place fast, she'd remembered that photo in the newspaper and had acted without thinking. Though she wouldn't follow through with her plan to find Jeff, she wasn't sorry they'd come to this beautiful spot.

After their meal, followed by ice cream, they walked back to the car, making slow progress with so many tourists about. Out of the corner of her eye Gabi saw a crowd of people with children gathered around one of the rangers near the parking lot. Above their heads she could see his trademark hat.

As she made her way toward the Honda, Ashley cried, "Look at that cute dog, Mommy! He has pointy ears."

Gabi *was* looking…at the uniformed man. Though he was half-turned from her, she realized he must be the same ranger she'd seen in the paper with his dog. He had the animal on a leash now, while the kids took turns patting his head.

"I want to pet him, too." Ashley, who'd been begging for a dog, broke free and rushed forward. Gabi hurried to catch up.

"His name's Sergei," she heard the ranger say to one of the children.

"Does he kill bears?" another child asked.

"No. His job is to scare them away from the camp-grounds."

"But he's not very big."

At Ashley's comment, the ranger turned. "He doesn't need to be." Beneath the brim of his hat Gabi caught the glint of intelligent hazel eyes framed by well-shaped eyebrows dark as rich loam. As his head lifted, his hard-boned facial features became visible. The cleft in his chin was painfully familiar.

"Jeff!" She gave an involuntary cry, but he heard her. His gaze shifted from her daughter's face to her's. For a moment the two of them stared at one another, while the world whisked her away to a different time, when they'd been different people. It was Jeff, but the boy next door had grown from an attractive teenager into a tough, virile male whose presence shook her to the foundations.

"It really *is* you." His voice had a deeper timbre than she remembered.

This wasn't supposed to have happened, but it was too late now. "I was thinking the same thing about you. Who would have guessed you'd become a park ranger?"

Even though she'd already seen his picture in the paper, it was still a surprise to realize that being a ranger was what he did for a living. Back in Alhambra he'd talked about owning his own construction company one day.

With the children concentrated on the dog, she and Jeff seemed to be alone for the moment.

"Funny what life throws you when you had other plans."

"Yes," she said, out of breath.

"You must have just come from the beach." His glance took in Ashley, then he stared at Gabi again. "You and your daughter not only look alike, you have the same golden glow. Where's your husband?"

A logical question. "I'm divorced," Gabi answered, trying desperately not to show any emotion. What a joke, when she was terrified of what Ryan planned to do.

Jeff studied her with a hint of compassion. "I'm sorry to hear that. The last time I talked to Bev, she said you were happily married."

Jeff had talked to Bev? She'd never said a word about it to Gabi. It must have been ages ago, before Ashley was conceived.

"Sometimes the best marriages can go wrong. What about you? Do you have one or two little offshoots running around here somewhere?" She didn't see a wedding band, but not every married man chose to wear one.

"No."

No? Just no? Not even a "not yet"?

She had a hard time believing that. He was too attractive...too wonderful to still be single. Maybe his spouse had died, or maybe he was divorced, too, but saw no reason to divulge information that was none of

Gabi's business. Soon after Jeff had disappeared from her life, his father and stepmom, Ellen, had suddenly moved from Alhambra, causing Gabi to lose her only link to him.

The assumption that the grown-up Jeff had a wife and children now was one of the reasons she'd changed her mind about seeking him out here. After a tension-filled lull in the conversation, he looked down at her daughter. "Aren't you going to introduce us?"

Gabi struggled to calm her breath. "Ashley's my one and only. Honey, this is Jeff Thompson, an old friend of mine."

Ashley turned away from the dog and looked up at him with interest. Gabi could read her daughter's mind. He was a tall, imposing, uniformed park ranger, after all, and he had a dog that could scare off bears. "Hi."

"Hi, yourself, Ashley." His compelling smile hadn't changed. Gabi's heart fluttered as fast as a humming-bird's wings. "Your mother and I used to live next door to each other. In fact, I knew her from the time she was fourteen years old. I knew Monte and Nora, too."

He was referring to the two other foster children who'd lived there at the time, but Ashley wouldn't have known either of them. Gabi had helped tend cute little Monte, who'd been seven years younger. Nora had been Jeff's age, whereas Gabi had been a year younger. At times it got ugly because Jeff had been interested in her instead of Nora, whose jealousy had caused problems.

Ashley flicked her a surprised glance. "Which house?" Gabi had taken Ashley to visit Bev a couple of times.

"The pink one," Jeff answered for her. "Do you know you look a lot like your mother when she was younger, only your eyes are pure blue? Hers have some purple in them."

Heat swamped Gabi's cheeks. "How's your father?"

"He's much better since they divorced. Dad lives in Glendale. I visit him when I can."

"The next time you see him, say hello from me. I really liked your parents. They were always wonderful to me."

The memories were assailing her fast and furiously, bringing back remembered pain from when Jeff had left home for good. Gabi's agony had been so total it had taken several years before she'd started dating. Though it had happened ages ago, it seemed like yesterday. She didn't dare stay here talking to him any longer.

"Please don't let us keep you from your audience," she said, because he hadn't replied. "Ashley and I were just going to our car."

She couldn't handle this unexpected reunion. Whatever had made her think she could? Years ago, he'd left Alhambra without a word to her. No follow-up letter or postcard. No phone call. *Nothing.*

"Come on, honey." She gripped Ashley's hand and they started walking.

To her chagrin, Jeff followed them to the Honda, parked a half-dozen cars away. His dog rubbed his head against Ashley's legs, making her laugh in delight. "Are you staying in the park?" Jeff's quiet question snaked its way inside.

"No." Like him, Gabi chose not to give any more

information of a personal nature, and pulled the keys out of her purse to unlock the car. Ashley climbed in the backseat and strapped herself in. Gabi shut the door and got in front. "We're on a trip and decided to drive through to Yosemite Valley to get a bite to eat before moving on." It was a version of the truth.

She started the engine before looking at him. "You work in a spectacular place. Everyone should be so lucky. It was nice seeing you again. Take care, Jeff."

"You, too." A tiny nerve throbbed at the side of his mouth, the way it used to sometimes. It brought back a memory of her kissing it. So many memories. Too many.

"I wish we could get a dog like that," Ashley said as they backed up and drove away. Gabi could see Jeff in the rearview mirror, staring after them. Another turn of the wheel and then he was gone from her vision.

Unlike before when he'd gone away and she'd had no idea of his destination, she knew where she could find him now, but the knowledge did her no good. In fact, she knew it would always haunt her.

"So do I, honey, but the landlord has rules. Maybe one day soon we'll be able to move to a house, and then we'll buy one."

Ashley wasn't the only one with a wish. Gabi could wish life were different and the three of them lived together in a house with a dog. She would give anything in the world if Jeff could help them and make that dream come true.

Chapter Two

Jeff returned to headquarters on the double, with Sergei running to keep up with him. How long had Gabi been divorced?

If he approached Bev White, she'd refuse to talk to him. After Jeff's father and Ellen had moved to Glendale, there was no way to learn any information about Gabi. Jeff had visited several times since his father's divorce last year, but they'd stayed away from painful subjects like Jeff's mother dying or Jeff's being forced to leave home because of Gabi.

When he and Sergei entered the building, Jeff headed straight for Security. Ranger Finlay looked up from the computer.

"Hey, Jeff. I heard Chief Rossiter talking about Cal's wedding. It must have really been something."

"It was." But Jeff had forgotten all about it because his mind was suddenly on something else. "I need some information pronto."

"Sure. What is it?"

"Take this license-plate number and run it through the database." He dictated it to Finlay. "I need to know the name of the ranger who entered it in the system, the entrance and all the details you can give me on the driver of the vehicle."

His adrenaline had kicked into overdrive. Needing to do something with his excess energy, he gave Sergei a rubdown while he waited.

"Here it is, put in by Ranger Ness at the South Entrance at two-thirty this afternoon. Gabi Rafferty, age thirty-one, five foot six, blue eyes, dark hair, home address Rosemead, California, 4120 Laurelhurst Lane. Owner of a Honda Civic, valid driver's license, no tickets, no warrants out for her arrest."

"Did she make reservations in the park?"

He shook his head.

"Thanks."

Jeff wheeled around and headed for his office. After shutting the door he phoned Merrill, who'd be going off duty any minute now. *Come on. Pick up.*

"This is Ranger Ness."

"It's Jeff."

"Hey—I was hoping to hear from you. Are you in for our card game tonight?"

"I'm afraid I can't. I'm calling for some information."

"You sound kind of fierce. What's up?"

Fierce didn't begin to cover it. "There was a thirty-one-year-old woman with short, dark hair who came through on your watch at two-thirty today. She had a daugh—"

"Say no more. I remember *her*." His whistle carried through the phone line. "To be honest, she'd be impossible to forget." *That was truer than Merrill knew.* "What do you want to know?"

"When you asked her where she'd be staying, what did she say?"

"She didn't have reservations. I told her she'd better try to make one outside the park just in case nothing was available for tonight."

"So did she?"

"Yeah. I suggested several places, including the Travelodge in El Portal. She was able to get a room there."

Relief swept through Jeff that he wouldn't have to wait until his next day off, and drive all the way to Rosemead. "Thanks, Merrill."

"You're welcome." After a pause he added, "Are you okay?"

Jeff sensed the other ranger wanted to ask him why he needed that information, but didn't want to probe. "After I attend to something, I will be. Talk to you later." He hung up. "Come on, Sergei. We're off duty. Let's go home. I need a shower and shave before we leave the park."

Jeff didn't care how many years had gone by; certain behavior never changed. Gabi had been so unlike the girl he'd once known, he'd sensed instinctively something was wrong. Divorce could do bad things to people.

If she'd been divorced only a short time, it might account for the fact that her nerves were fragile. He could never remember her being so quiet. In all the time he'd known her, they'd never run out of things to talk about. There'd been no awkward moments.

Today that's all there had been on her part—awkward moments punctuated with pauses and averted eyes. She was a California girl and knew you didn't go anywhere without making a reservation first. It didn't add up that she'd come to Yosemite, of all places, without any forethought. Just passing through? He didn't buy her explanation.

After heating up a couple enchiladas in the micro-wave, he downed them with a cup of coffee before leaving in the truck with Sergei. This time of the evening traffic wasn't quite so bad driving out of the park. He could make up time and hopefully find her in El Portal before she went to bed.

Her little girl looked so much like her, especially her eyes and rosebud mouth, that she'd stolen Jeff's heart. They had the same shaped heads and dark, curly hair like gypsies. *Incredible.* Those save-the-whales shirts reminded him of Gabi's old T-shirts. She'd always filled them out to perfection. While political slogans had intrigued her, Gabi's shape had intrigued him. So had her inquiring mind. He'd loved her company. They'd been inseparable.

He frowned as he reflected on her quick departure from the parking lot. "Goodbye, Jeff." *That was it?* When you hadn't even said a meaningful hello, you didn't just walk away from an old friend you'd had a history with!

Except that he'd done the exact same thing to her when he'd been forced to walk away from her years ago. He'd had no choice, after making promises to his father and Bev White not to contact her. At the time he'd been in so much pain, he hadn't considered what Gabi might be going through. His dad had told him Gabi was still so young, she'd get over him fast.

All Jeff knew was that the next time he heard anything about her, she was married, which proved his father right. The knowledge that she had a husband shouldn't have come as such a blow, but it did.... Jeff's own marriage to Fran happened on the heels of that information.

What a mistake that had been! So unfair to his ex-wife. To his chagrin, she got in touch with him from time to time, insisting she would always love him. He kept hoping that the next time she called, it would be to tell him she was getting married again.

Jeff shook his head. What were the odds of him running into Gabi at the park? The coincidence was so astounding he could hardly credit it.

This morning at the wedding ceremony he'd felt chills, and he was feeling them even stronger now. Gabi had been on his mind just hours before he'd looked up to see her staring at him. The color of her eyes hadn't changed. The purple flecks reminded him of the dainty purple violets growing in the grass at the edge of Bridal-veil Meadow.

At quarter to ten he reached the motel and spotted her car in the parking lot. "You stay put, Sergei. I'll be back." After locking the truck, he went inside the Travelodge to the front desk, where an attractive redhead looked up and smiled at him as she took in his uniform.

"Hi. What can I do for you?"

"Good evening. A Mrs. Rafferty from Rosemead, California, made a reservation for her and her daughter today. It couldn't have been a long time since they checked in. Would you please ring her room and tell her Ranger Thompson needs to speak to her?"

The redhead gave him a speculative glance. "Sure. Just a minute." She consulted the computer before picking up the phone. After a few seconds he heard her explain to Gabi why she was calling. Her eyes played over him after she hung up. "You're to call her on the in-house phone in the hallway to your left. Just dial 018."

"Thank you."

"You're welcome," she answered, with another provocative smile.

He found the phone kiosk and punched the digits. In a moment Gabi picked up. "Jeff?" Her same voice, yet she was tentative, hesitant.

"I was still on duty when you drove away, but I'm free now. If you're putting Ashley to bed, I'll wait by the phone until you call me back."

"She's asleep."

Good. "I'm not surprised. You've driven a long way today." He waited for more response from her.

She took a sharp breath. In that instant he thought he sensed anger. "The park must have an amazing security system for you to have found me."

"Threats of terrorism have made it mandatory."

"Am I being investigated?" She was so tense, she'd lost her sense of humor.

"Yes," he teased, "but you sound tired, so I'll let you go now and we'll talk in the morning over breakfast." Jeff figured the woman at the desk could find him a room for tonight.

"I won't be here." Her reply was brittle.

His hand tightened on the phone. "Why not?"

"Ashley and I are going to spend a few days in San Francisco."

Gabi was lying through her teeth. "You mean you don't have an hour in the morning for two old friends to take a walk down memory lane before you leave?"

"You mean the way you didn't have an hour in the morning for two old friends to talk before you left Alhambra for good?"

His jaw clenched. "There was a reason for that."

"I know. You'd just graduated from high school and wanted to get on with the rest of your life. I do understand. Honestly. Now I'm asking for *your* understanding. If I stay on the phone any longer, Ashley will wake up."

"Then I'll meet you outside your door, where we won't disturb her."

"I can't. I'm too exhausted and we have to get an early start in the morning."

He wasn't about to let this go. "For your daughter's sake, you'll have to eat something first. I'll meet you in the restaurant. Tell me a time."

"I'm not sure."

Which could mean she had no intention of eating breakfast there at all. In that case, he'd keep an eye on her car. "Good night, Gabi. Sleep well."

Sleep well?

Jeff's comment guaranteed she'd lie awake again all night. There was no use trying to run away from him. He'd left the park to come after her. His determination to talk to her would make it pretty well impossible for her to elude him no matter how hard she tried.

She knew he'd be outside in the morning waiting for her. The only sensible thing to do would be to face him. She'd get him talking about his life. Should her attorney phone while she was in the restaurant, she'd excuse herself to take the call. Otherwise she would say goodbye to Jeff after they'd eaten, and head for San Francisco.

After getting off the phone, she thought she'd never sleep, but she was wrong. Probably because she'd given in to the inevitable where Jeff was concerned, she relaxed enough to let go of her fears for a little while and find oblivion.

But having always been an early riser, she awakened at six-thirty the next morning unable to fight a growing excitement, because she knew she'd be seeing Jeff one more time. She'd brought all this on by driving to Yosemite in the first place. Naturally, she needed to be the one to end it ASAP.

Once she'd showered and changed into fresh jeans and a short-sleeved blouse in a blue-and-green print, it was Ashley's turn to get ready. Gabi put her in white shorts and a kelly-green knit top with white polka dots. They both wore white sandals.

"Let's take the suitcases out to the car, then go to the restaurant."

"Okay. Can I have cereal and apple juice?"

"That sounds good to me, too. Come on."

They left the room and walked out to the parking lot. As Gabi was stowing their bags in the trunk, Ashley pulled on her arm. "Your old friend's here, Mom. He brought his dog."

Gabi shut the trunk lid and looked around in time to

see a bareheaded Jeff coming toward them. His dark brown hair was cropped shorter than he used to wear it, making it wavy rather than curly like hers. With his complexion burnished from being in the sun, and his lean, powerful physique, he put every other male out of the competition.

A wide smile greeted them. Her "old friend" was such a sensational-looking male in uniform that if Gabi were the type to keel over, she'd be on the ground by now. She imagined even fit men would kill to have his build, one that came from living in the out-of-doors year-round.

In high school her girlfriend Kim had referred to Jeff as the ultimate stud. On his Kawasaki motorcycle, he could have been the company's poster boy. If Kim, who was married and lived in Oregon, could see him now, she'd be speechless.

"It appears Sergei and I got back from our walk just in time. How would you ladies like to join me for breakfast on the patio?"

"Could we, Mom?" Ashley begged, clearly eager to play with the dog.

"That sounds good."

The four of them walked around to an alcove that led to the terrace overlooking the Merced River. Tourists had started filling up the tables. A waitress seated them and took their orders.

"I wish a bear would come so we could watch Sergei scare it away."

Laughter broke from Jeff, the rich kind Gabi remembered, though it hadn't been as deep back then. The leap from teenager to manly man had wrought striking changes she was still trying to absorb.

"Has he had his breakfast?" Ashley asked.

"Not yet. He'll eat after I take him home in a little while, but he enjoyed a nice drink at the river."

"Did it cost a lot to buy a dog like him?"

Jeff leaned forward. "I don't know what he cost. He's not my dog."

"Did you find him?"

Ashley was so dear and so curious, Gabi couldn't help smiling. Neither could Jeff, apparently.

"I'm babysitting him for my best friend."

"Where does your friend live?"

"In the park near my house. His name is Ranger Hollis. He's on his honeymoon."

Ashley turned to her mom. "What's that?" she asked in a quiet voice.

Gabi stirred in her seat, wishing the subject hadn't come up. "It sounds like Ranger Hollis just got married and went on a trip with his new wife."

"Oh." Gabi could hear the wheels turning. "Did you go on a honeymoon with my daddy?"

"I did," she answered, before taking a drink of water.

"Where did you go?"

Enough with the questions. "Catalina Island."

"I know where that is." Ashley's head whipped around in Jeff's direction. "Did you go on a honeymoon?"

"A short one to Carmel, but our marriage didn't last long and we got divorced."

Carmel... A divine place Gabi had only seen in films. She couldn't look at him.

"So did my mommy."

"Here's our breakfast, honey." *Thank heaven.*

Jeff had ordered eggs and bacon. He dug in with a healthy appetite. After Ashley had eaten most of her cornflakes she looked at him. "Could I feed Sergei some of your toast?"

"The dog isn't allowed table food, but I've got a doggy treat you can give him." Jeff reached in his pocket. "Before you let him have it, ask him to shake your hand."

Ashley giggled and slid off the chair. She went around to the dog, which lay at Jeff's feet. "Shake my hand," she told him. Gabi watched in delight as the dog lifted his paw to her daughter, who giggled again before feeding him the treat.

For a moment Gabi gazed into hazel eyes lit with a tender glint. She'd seen that look before. It melted her heart. This was madness. Jeff meant nothing to her anymore, and her happiness was being threatened in a very real way back in Rosemead. Yet here she was, enjoying this moment more than anything she'd experienced in years.

"Why the rush to leave Yosemite when you've barely arrived?"

The low-pitched question—straight and to the point—came out so unexpectedly, it caught Gabi off guard. Her nervous glance slid to Ashley, who was still hunkered down and too busy petting the dog to have heard him.

Gabi lowered her head. "I don't know what you're tal—"

"There's a reason you came to Yosemite on the fly,"

he interrupted without a qualm. Gabi decided his confidence was a trait he'd been born with. "Admit you were never on your way to San Francisco."

At his stunning perception, she caught her breath. He heard her and a satisfied expression broke out on his face. "You're in some kind of trouble. Since I'm here, why not tell me what it is? Maybe I can help."

His comment sent her heart into a full gallop. To her dismay it was exacerbated by the ringing of her phone. Maybe it was her attorney. Her composure shattered, she dropped the spoon she'd been using into her cereal bowl with a clatter, before reaching for her purse.

Jeff's eyes never left her face as she pulled out her cell and checked the caller ID. It was Greg Sorenson, the head of third-grade curriculum in her school district. Divorced and interested in dating, he'd taken her and Ashley out to dinner before they'd left for the beach. He expected Gabi home in another day and no doubt wanted to see her as soon as she arrived. She ignored the call, deciding to phone him later, when she was alone.

"Who was that, Mommy?"

She finished her juice before answering. "Greg."

"Oh."

"Who's Greg?" Jeff asked Ashley.

"Mommy's friend."

Before he could ask another question, the phone rang again. This time it was Bev. Gabi turned in the chair for privacy.

"Bev?"

"Are you still away from home?"

"Yes. What's happened?"

"Ryan just called me again, demanding to know where you are. When I told him I didn't have the faintest idea, he said he would hire a private investigator to find you because he wanted to see his child. When he hung up, he almost broke my eardrum doing it."

Gabi winced. "I'm so sorry he's gotten you involved. As soon as we hang up I'll call my attorney and see what he can do so you're not harassed."

"It's Ashley he's after."

"Since he wanted nothing to do with her before, I don't understand this, but I'll take care of it so he doesn't contact you anymore, Bev. I promise." She rang off, to discover Jeff's piercing gaze still focused on her.

"You've gone pale, Gabi." He put some bills on the table and stood up. That roused Sergei, who sprang to his feet. Jeff looked down at Ashley. "Would you like to walk the dog around outside?"

Excitement lit up her face. "Can I, Mommy?"

"Sergei is wonderful with children and will stay right by her," Jeff assured Gabi.

She tried to calm down, but it was a losing battle. "For a few minutes, but then we have to go."

Jeff gave her daughter the leash. Ashley couldn't have been more delighted. The four of them started walking. It was a relief to leave the restaurant, where they'd been surrounded by an audience. The sight of a park ranger with a dog made anonymity impossible. The last thing Gabi wanted was to create a scene.

"Stay on the grass bordering the parking lot, honey."

"I will."

The moment Ashley was out of earshot, Jeff moved

closer. "Will you answer me one question? I promise it has nothing to do with your phone call or your turmoil, neither of which are any of my business."

His sincerity defeated her, but she was afraid to look him in the eye for fear she'd reveal too much. "What is it?"

"Would you have stayed in the park last night if there'd been a vacancy?" When she hesitated, he added, "Provided you hadn't seen me?" He'd always been good at reading minds. Nothing got past him.

"Yes," she admitted at last. "Ashley was so tired I hated the idea of having to get back in the car and do more driving."

He cocked his head. "On the heels of that thought, she won't like another drive to San Francisco this morning, so I've got an idea. If you'll follow me back to the park, I'll lead you to a place where I can guarantee a reservation for as long as you need one. What are friends for, after all."

His remark captured Gabi's attention. She studied him for a moment. "That's a very generous offer. If every ranger was as accommodating to an old friend, there'd be no lodgings for the regular tourists."

A ghost of a smile hovered on his lips. "I'm not just any ranger."

Gabi chuckled quietly in spite of the tension. "No. In that newspaper article beneath the picture it said you were the chief stew—" She stopped midsentence, but too late to catch herself. Her face went hot as a blowtorch.

"You're referring to the one where I'm standing next

to Alex Harcourt. She's the bride on the honeymoon with Ranger Hollis."

Jeff had just cleared up any question Gabi had been secretly harboring since last month. He'd read her mind with his usual uncanny clarity.

"She sounds like a remarkable woman, to have funded those Zuni volunteer teenagers with her own money."

"She grew up loving them, and wanted to give them a unique experience, which makes her even more remarkable. But I'd rather talk about you and Ashley right now. Let me put a question to you. If I unexpectedly turned up on your doorstep on a hot day, wouldn't you invite me in for a cold drink before I went on my way?" He held up his palm. "Be careful how you answer. Remember, I lived next door to you for three years."

She'd never forgotten. Jeff had been an integral part of her life until he'd gone away. After she met Ryan, she'd tried to bury those memories, but had been unsuccessful.

"I know you're in trouble of some kind, but I promise not to pry into your personal affairs. All I want to do is be a friend, because you look as if you need one."

"Is it that obvious?"

"Only to me," he said in a husky tone, "but that's because we spent so much time together and I see certain signs. After all these years, I'm glad you felt you could still come to me, even if you decided to change your mind at the last minute."

With her secret exposed, Gabi had no choice but to be honest with him now. "Two nights ago Bev received a threatening phone call from my ex-husband, while I was vacationing at Oceanside with Ashley. What he said frightened me so terribly, I called my attorney, Henry Steel. After telling me not to go home or to Bev's house, he advised me to find a safe place until he'd talked to my ex-husband's attorney.

"I'd remembered seeing the picture of you at Yosemite. Suddenly that sounded like a safe place, and I found myself seeking you out, but it was irrational of me. Once Ashley and I reached the Yosemite Valley and there were no vacancies, I came to my senses and told her we were leaving for El Portal. But she saw the dog and then I saw *you*. We were well and truly caught."

Lines bracketed his mouth. "So if she hadn't seen Sergei, the two of you would have left?"

"Yes," Gabi answered honestly, and saw the way his brows furrowed. "After that phone call from my attorney, I went out of my mind for a little while. Until Ashley and I reached Curry Village, I didn't realize how delusional I was being for even coming to the park. It was sheer lunacy on my part to think a person I'd known way back in high school would want to be approached."

"I was hardly just any person, Gabi," he insisted.

"True. You were my next-door neighbor in my youth, but it's been fourteen years since the last time I…said good-night to you in the driveway, after that movie. You can't make me feel better for my impulsiveness, Jeff. In fact, I'm so embarrassed I could cry. But I'm a mother and have to act like one, or Ashley will be more upset than she already is."

Except that right now her daughter looked as if she

was having a marvelous time, running around with the dog.

"Is she frightened, too?"

Gabi shook her head. "No, but since that phone call at the beach, she senses something's wrong."

He shifted his weight. "You need a place where she can play and you can relax, while you deal with this emergency. Agreed?"

"Yes."

"Then I don't see a problem. After you follow me back to the park, I have to go on duty. You'll have a place to yourself for as long as you need, to talk to your attorney and deal with this crisis."

"You swear it won't put you out?"

His keen gaze trapped hers. "I *am* an old friend. It will grieve me if you refuse this small thing I can do for you."

"Thank you, Jeff," she whispered. But alongside her relief, warning bells went off, because she could never look at him as just a friend. It wasn't possible. "I'll do this only if you let me pay you."

"That's fine." He glanced at her daughter. "While you get Ashley, I'll load Sergei and we'll leave. On our way we'll be passing through the Arch Rock Entrance. When we get there, the ranger will ask you the usual questions. Just play tourist and answer them the same way you did with the other ranger yesterday. No more, no less."

Gabi nodded. She understood. Though she might be following him back into the park, he didn't want anyone else to know that. He wasn't interested in her romantically. The last thing he needed was any of his colleagues jumping to an erroneous conclusion, especially if he was involved with another woman right now. Jeff was divorced, and she couldn't blame him for wanting to avoid unnecessary gossip.

Chapter Three

Jeff nodded to Matt Wilson, the ranger at the entrance to the park. He wanted to tell the other man that Gabi was with him and didn't need to be stopped to answer questions, but he didn't dare. The grapevine reached everywhere.

It was bad enough Ranger Ness had witnessed Jeff's strange behavior yesterday concerning one Gabi Rafferty driving a blue Honda Civic. He didn't relish another ranger speculating on the gorgeous black-haired beauty and her relationship to Jeff.

He pulled to the side of the road and watched through the rearview mirror until she'd answered the usual questions and passed through. The dog sat up on the seat next to him. Jeff ruffled his fur.

"Little did you know you're going to have a new playmate, Sergei. For how long, I have no idea. We're going to take this an hour at a time, okay, buddy?" As Gabi drove out, Jeff pulled onto the road again directly in front of her.

There was no time like the present to get things set up. He rang Chief Rossiter's house. After three rings his wife, Rachel, answered.

"Hi, Jeff. Seems kind of strange around here without Cal or Alex, doesn't it?"

It had, until he'd lifted his head yesterday and had stared into a pair of divine blue eyes tinged with purple.

"I'm sure it feels that way to Sergei. I was wondering what Nicky's doing later on this morning."

She laughed. "Besides driving me crazy?"

Jeff smiled. "Do you think he'd like to come over and bring his dog? A family friend from way back, Gabi Rafferty, and her seven-year-old daughter, Ashley, will be staying at my house today while I'm on duty. Since she and Nicky both love dogs, I think the two of them would get along great. I'll make sure they eat lunch. What do you think?"

"Nicky will love it!"

"Good."

"It will be nice for him to play with someone close to his own age. He's missing being with his school friends. Most every family has taken a vacation this August."

Ashley had just come from one and was probably missing her friends, too, especially under circumstances Jeff had yet to understand. "I'm driving in from El Portal and will call you when I reach the house."

"Perfect. I'll tell him to take his binoculars and a couple of board games along."

"Terrific. Thanks, Rachel."

"Thank you. It will give me some alone time with the baby. Talk to you later."

After they'd hung up, he rang Bryce and told him he wouldn't be able to join him at the site until tomorrow. For the rest of the day Jeff intended to remain at headquarters and get caught up on paperwork, then head home early and fix dinner.

He hadn't entertained anyone since moving in. In his wildest dreams he couldn't have imagined Gabi being his first guest. Her last name had been White before she got married, because it had been Bev's last name. Before that she'd had other last names. Gabi wasn't her birth name, either. Her first foster parent had named her that.

She'd had so many painful changes in her young life before and after she came to live with the White family, yet there was no one more resilient. Despite Nora's mean-spirited nature and jealousy of Jeff's interest in her, Gabi took it in stride. She never felt sorry for herself.

Her forward-looking attitude was something he especially loved about her. But his plan to marry her and make her feel secure and safe one day had blown up in his face because she'd wed someone else.

He shouldn't have been so hurt that she could fall in love with another guy. Somehow he'd thought her feelings for him had run as deep as his for her. Not true. End of story until yesterday, when Gabi's troubled divorce had planted her and her daughter squarely in Jeff's private world. It was a scenario he would never have imagined.

Cal would probably tell him he was a fool to have gone after her last evening, but fourteen years ago Jeff had been forced to leave Gabi without explanation. This might be the only chance he would ever get to reveal the circumstances that led up to his going away without warning. If she needed help, he was prepared to offer it.

Jeff had been a grown man for a long time now. No threats from Bev White, or his father telling him what to do, could touch him. Neither of them had any say about his life.

GABI KEPT HER EYES on Jeff's truck as they entered Yosemite Valley, trying to anticipate when he would stop. The morning traffic was worse than last evening's.

"Are we going to stay at that big hotel? On the paper it says the Ah-wah-nee."

"I don't know, honey. Ranger Thompson said to follow him, so that's what I'm doing." Instinct told her he was taking her to wherever he lived.

They drove past the park's headquarters and pretty soon he turned onto a road that led to a cluster of houses. They looked like the kind built in the 1950s. There were subdivisions of ranch-style houses like them everywhere in California. He drove two blocks before turning into a driveway on the left.

The garage door went up. She spotted a red-and-black motorcycle at the far end and a gray Volvo parked on the left side. He'd always had a fascination for fast cars and bikes.

Jeff climbed down from his truck and walked over to her door. "Go ahead and drive on in."

Gabi shook her head. "We can't stay at your house."

"Sure you can. You're paying me, right? It's the only

room in town." He said it with a smile for Ashley. Gabi realized he meant it literally.

"Jeff—"

"Don't look now," he interrupted, "but the chief ranger's son is rounding the corner with his mutt. He's come to play with your daughter." As he said it, he opened the rear door for Ashley to jump down. Sergei rushed to rub his body against her, making her laugh. "Here." He handed her the leash. "Let him walk around in the front yard."

"Okay. Come on, Sergei," Ashley cried with excitement, behaving as if he was her dog already.

With the die cast, Gabi had little choice but to enter the garage. Jeff followed. "Pop the trunk."

She did his bidding so he could retrieve the two suitcases. After he'd shut the lid, he waited for her to join him in the driveway. By now the boy's little white dog had run over to Sergei, making yapping noises.

"Hi, Nicky!"

"Hi, Jeff!"

"I'm glad you could come to my house. This is Ashley Rafferty and her mom, Gabi, from Rosemead. We're old friends."

"Then how come they never came before?"

Gabi noticed Jeff trying not to laugh. "Because we lost touch until they arrived at the park yesterday."

Gabi couldn't help smiling at the darling blond-haired boy wearing a backpack. "Hello, Nicky."

"Hi."

"Hi!" Ashley spoke up. "What's your dog's name?"

"Samson. He's really Samson the second. My dad

had the first Samson, but he died and Dad buried him at his grandparents' house in Oakhurst. My grandparents live there now."

"Oh," Ashley said, obviously surprised by such a long speech. "I don't even have a dog."

Jeff patted her shoulder. "You can pretend Sergei is yours while you're here." Ashley beamed in response.

Nicky eyed her with interest. "Did you know he's a Karelian bear dog from Finland?"

"Yes. Ranger Thompson told me."

"Sergei belongs to Ranger Hollis."

"I know. He's on his honeymoon."

"Dad says he's lucky."

"Did your dad go on a honeymoon?"

"Yup. I went with him."

"Where did you go?"

"We went to London. I got to see where Harry Potter took the train to Hogwarts. Have you ever heard of Harry Potter?"

"Of course. I have Hedwig pajamas."

He studied her with new appreciation. "What grade are you in?"

"I'll be going into second."

"So will Brittany, but she's on vacation right now."

"Who's Brittany?"

"She's our teacher's daughter."

"Oh."

"I'll be in third grade. Do you want to look through my binoculars later? If we're real quiet, you can see a California woodpecker in that black oak across the street. Jeff says it digs for acorns out of a pit it dug for itself."

Ashley stared up at Jeff. "Does it really do that?"

He crossed his heart. "But to catch him eating, you have to wait till it's getting dark."

"Will you be able to stay till then?" Gabi's daughter asked Nicky.

"I think so. I'll have to call my mom. If I can't, do you want to come over to my house and see my new baby brother? His name is Parker."

"Yes, but don't you have to ask your dad if it's all right?"

"Nope. He's too busy being the chief of the *whole park*."

"Is it big?"

"It's *huge*."

"Tell you what, guys," Jeff interjected. "We're going in the house." Gabi felt he was purposely not looking at her. "You can come inside whenever you want."

By tacit agreement she followed him back to the garage, and on into the house. He closed the garage door on the way into the kitchen and set her suitcases on the floor. By now he'd broken into laughter. It mingled with hers until they both had tears in their eyes.

She couldn't remember the last time she'd laughed this hard. Maybe not since she'd last seen Jeff, who found humor in everything. "That Nicky has to be the funniest, cutest boy I ever met in my life, and I've taught hundreds of them."

Jeff's laughter died down. He studied her intently. "What do you mean?"

"I'm a schoolteacher in Rosemead. Third grade."

"I thought you wanted to go into social work."

"As you said earlier, life has a way of changing

one's preconceived notions. Teaching has allowed me to be with Ashley as much as possible. She's my whole world."

He was so quiet, she realized there was a lot to digest. Eventually he asked, "How long have you been divorced?"

Gabi held on to the back of one of the wooden chairs. "Close to eight years."

She watched his eyes darken. They only did that when emotion gripped him. "Then you were still pregnant when you separated?"

Remembered pain stabbed her. "Yes. When I told Ryan we were expecting a baby, he told me he didn't want children."

"You didn't know that before you married him?" Jeff asked incredulously.

"We'd planned to wait a few years before starting a family, but Ashley came along anyway. Ryan's reaction to the pregnancy was to insist I get an abortion immediately."

Jeff's lips thinned.

"It was a nightmarish time for me." Jeff didn't need to hear details. She didn't want him to know. "I told Ryan it was out of the question. Bev told me to go to the YWCA. That's what I did. They put me in a shelter and helped me find a divorce lawyer. I filed, and it wasn't long before Ryan was deployed to Japan. I never had contact with him again."

A strange sound came out of Jeff's throat. "You mean he never made arrangements to see his own flesh and blood?"

"No. He signed away his parental rights."

Jeff folded his arms as if he needed to do something with them.

"I worked at a job until Ashley was born. Then I paid a woman to help tend her until I found an opening at an elementary school in Rosemead. After I was hired, I moved there to an apartment, put my baby in day care, and that's been my life until two nights ago, when Ryan called Bev out of the blue. He said he was home from the military and wanted to see our child."

"So he's now decided he doesn't want to agree to the divorce stipulation."

"I'm afraid so. When Bev reminded him he'd given up his parental rights, he claimed his attorney would see about that. I called my old attorney. He told me to get to a safe place with Ashley until he'd had a chance to talk to Ryan's lawyer."

She moistened her lips nervously. "It was a good thing I didn't go home after we left the beach. He called Bev again with a message for me."

"What was that?"

"He was hiring a private investigator to find me, and there wasn't a thing I could do about it."

Jeff's all-seeing gaze traveled over her. "You're trembling. What did he do to you during your marriage, Gabi? Your attorney wouldn't have told you to find a safe place unless you were in danger."

"Ryan didn't beat me up, if that's what you're thinking." She took a quick breath. "But he did get rough and verbally abusive when I refused to consider an abortion. It was a dark side of him that frightened me because it was so unexpected."

"You never saw that behavior manifested before you married him?"

"No. Never."

"He's definitely mentally disturbed in some way."

She nodded. "When Mr. Steel was drawing up the final papers, Ryan agreed to give up his parental rights in exchange for my not filing abuse charges that could go on his military record. I sold the diamond ring to help pay my attorney's expenses."

"How did you get the money for college?"

"Student loans and my catering job."

His body tautened. "You've had it tough."

"You're wrong, Jeff. I have a satisfying career, good friends who are colleagues and a wonderful daughter I love to death."

"How serious is it with Greg?"

Nothing ever got past Jeff. "I've dated him a couple times." *But he's not you, Jeff. No man is.* "Everything in my life has been going fine."

"Until now." His hands went to his hips in a totally masculine gesture. "Your attorney was right to tell you not to go home."

She lowered her head. "But I have to go at some point, and I had no right to make this your problem. My attorney should be phoning before the end of the day, and will advise me how to proceed."

"While you wait for his call, I'm going to run over to headquarters and get a little work done, but I'll be back early." He reached for a notepad and pen lying by the cordless phone on the counter.

"I've put down my cell-phone number and a few others, like Nicky's mother and the number at headquarters. Ranger Davis usually answers and will know where to find me if for some reason you can't reach me on my cell," Jeff said, before turning to her. "Call me if you need anything. I'll phone you later and check to see if everything's okay."

"I—I don't know how to thank you, Jeff." Gabi's voice faltered. "Asking Nicky to come over was very thoughtful."

"We're friends, remember?"

Yes, she remembered, but she'd thought his feelings had run deeper than that. Evidently they hadn't, or he wouldn't have vanished from her life like a burning star that had all of a sudden cooled and become invisible.

"My house is yours, Gabi. Make yourself comfortable." He reached into a cupboard and filled the dog dish with food, then replenished the water bowl. "Sergei will eat when he's ready. There's food and drinks in the fridge for you and the kids."

"We'll be fine."

"Tell me your cell number. I want to program it into my phone so we can stay in touch wherever you are."

She dictated it to him. He was the old Jeff, always concerned for her welfare. There was no one in the world like him. Whatever the reason for his divorce, the woman he'd married had gotten the prize of a lifetime. No matter what had caused their breakup, Gabi couldn't imagine his ex-wife ever getting over him.

Gabi followed him through the modest dining and living rooms to the front door. She watched him talk to the children for a minute before he climbed in his truck and drove off. Sergei seemed perfectly content to stay with Ashley. Knowing the dog was trained to chase bears away relieved her of any worry in that regard.

"When you guys get hungry or thirsty, come on in the kitchen!"

"Okay," they both answered, but Ashley was having fun watching Nicky, who could make the dogs do tricks. They were so carefree, the scene caught at Gabi's heart.

She closed the door, leaving it unlocked, and headed for the kitchen, where she'd left her purse and the suitcases.

The dark blue suede easy chairs in the living room looked attractive on either side of the tan leather couch. On the walls were two large colored photographs in white frames and matting. They dominated the room, taking her breath away.

One was of a Yosemite meadow filled with glorious spring wildflowers. The other was of a park waterfall in winter. Gabi didn't know which one. In the foreground were small clumps of ice in the river, like a slush drink. She'd never seen anything so beautiful or unusual.

In the bathroom he'd hung a small picture showing him and his parents out in front of their house. He must have been seventeen there, an inch taller than his dad. The photo would have been taken right before his mother was diagnosed with cancer and died. Gabi's eyes misted over. They looked happy. *Because they were...* She'd always hoped to have a home like theirs one day, where everyone seemed content.

Now that she had time to get her bearings, she discovered Jeff kept a tidy three-bedroom house. Nothing out of place. In Alhambra she'd been in his bedroom many a time. It had been messy, with clothes on the floor, a basketball in the wastebasket. She remembered lots of books lying on his unmade bed, a few posters hung haphazardly on his closet door. The only thing he'd kept neat was the top of his dresser, where he put his motorcycle helmet and leathers.

Ruth, Jeff's mother, hadn't been an anal housekeeper like Bev. She was easygoing. Gabi had liked spending time there, where the pace was slower. Ruth had done a lot of baking, and kept her husband and only son well fed. Gabi had liked to watch her cook, and learned a lot from her. She'd been the lucky recipient of many a delicious meal.

But the heart of their home for the men had been the Thompson garage. Jeff's father was in construction, and used one side of it as his workshop. The other included an enviable amount of tools, and Jeff's prized motorcycle. Gabi doubted they'd ever parked a car in there. She'd spent so much time looking at his motorcycle magazines, stacked in one corner, that he'd brought out a beanbag chair from their family room so she'd have a place to sit while he tinkered.

So many memories of a time that would never come again...

On her way back to the living room, Gabi peeked inside the door of his bedroom. If he had other pictures from his past, they weren't visible. The dark green quilt covering the queen-size bed had a fat white stripe running down it. He'd always liked green. When he rode around on his Kawasaki, he usually wore a hunter-green T-shirt. The color brought out the green flecks in his hazel eyes.

Gabi tossed her head back as if to clear it, and walked to the front door to see how the children were doing. When she looked out, four bodies, canine and human, lay in the grass. The children were looking up at cloud formations. Ashley held the binoculars. Nicky was a sweet boy to share them with her. It was a special moment.

Gabi ran back to the living room and pulled the cell phone from her purse. Before anyone moved, she stepped out onto the porch and took half a dozen pictures in succession.

Not wanting to disturb them, she went back inside and phoned her attorney, unable to wait any longer. His secretary said he was with a client, but would call her back. While Gabi waited, she called her friend Shelley, who lived in a condo across the street in Rosemead. She was married and had a daughter Ashley's age, named Jessica. They went to school together and had the same teacher.

Gabi knew Jessica was waiting for Ashley to come home from their trip. This would be a disappointing call, but there was no help for it. In a way, she was relieved to get Shelley's voice mail. That way she could explain they were extending their vacation a little longer, without having to answer any specific questions. She promised to be in touch later.

If there was the slightest chance a private investigator traced Gabi to Rosemead and did question Jessica if he saw her outside, she could say she didn't know anything.

One more phone message to leave, telling Greg she'd

be on vacation for a while longer and would let him know as soon as she got back.

Then, feeling at loose ends, she went back to the kitchen and found a jar of decaf on the shelf. There were clean dishes in the dishwasher. She pulled out a mug and fixed herself some coffee, which she heated in the microwave. A little more rummaging produced sugar.

She sat down at the kitchen table to drink it. Halfway through, her phone rang. Gabi checked the caller ID and clicked on. "Mr. Steel?" she said anxiously.

"Hello, Mrs. Rafferty. I'm sorry you had to call me first this morning. I've just been informed your husband has hired a different attorney, named James Durham. His secretary phoned my office a little while ago."

Her hand tightened on the phone. "Do you know him?"

"Yes."

"Is he good?"

"Yes, but we've got the law on our side." She shuddered. "He hasn't gotten back to me yet. As you know, these things can take time. Are you in a position where you can stay away a little longer?"

"Yes, but I'm concerned about Ryan bothering my foster mother."

"I'll let his attorney know that the phone calls and personal visits have to stop or his client will be slapped with harassment charges. That would ruin his case. It shouldn't be long now. Keep your spirits up."

"I will. Thank you, Mr. Steel."

She rang off and swallowed the rest of her coffee,

shivering at the idea of some P.I. finding her apartment so Ryan could creep around.

While there was still peace and quiet, she made half a dozen phone calls to find a place to stay in the park tonight. She finally managed to get a room at the Yosemite Lodge because of a cancellation. After one o'clock she could check in and pick up her key.

Gabi looked at her watch. It was almost that time now, except that she wouldn't be able to go over there yet. Sergei was her responsibility until Jeff got back. The dog needed to eat and so did the children.

She got busy making peanut-butter sandwiches and apple slices before calling them in to wash their hands. All four came running. In a few minutes they were gathered around the kitchen table. Nicky kept Samson by him while Sergei went for his food.

"Do you two want milk?"

"Could we please have root beer?" Nicky asked. "Jeff always keeps some for me and Roberta." That sounded like something Jeff would do.

"After your milk, two root beers will be coming up for dessert."

"Who's Roberta?" Ashley asked curiously.

He looked at her. "She's twelve, but she's still my friend. She has a beagle named Snoopy."

"I have one, too, but he's not real. His name is Mr. Charles."

Nicky laughed at the amusing name.

"Where does she live?" Ashley asked between bites of sandwich.

"Two blocks from here. Her dad helps my dad."

"Oh."

"What does *your* dad do?" Nicky took another bite of sandwich.

"I don't know."

Ashley needed some input about now. "Her father and I are divorced, Nicky. He went into the military a long time ago."

"My dad was a Marine in Iraq before he became the chief ranger."

"Oh," Ashley said again, obviously impressed by everything Nicky told her. It was hilarious.

"Roberta's mother is an archaeologist who works with another archaeologist, but he got divorced in Mexico and doesn't have any children. Are you sad your dad went away?" Nicky's conversation traveled all over the place.

"Sometimes." Ashley's comment was so unexpected, Gabi froze in place.

"My real daddy and mommy died in a storm way up on top of El Capitan," Nicky informed them. "You saw it when you drove into the Yosemite Valley. I was really sad until my aunt Rachel brought me to Yosemite to talk to the chief ranger about why they died."

"What happened to them?"

"They got caught in a storm and died of hypothermia."

"Oh." Ashley's voice trembled. "What's hypothermia?"

"It's when you get too cold, but Vance said they didn't have any pain."

"I bet you're glad about that. Who's Vance?"

"My new dad. When we came to the park, he told me I could call him that. We all loved each other and got married and went to England on our honeymoon. Now I'm their real son and I'm not sad anymore."

Gabi tried to swallow, but the swelling made her throat too tight.

Nicky drank some more milk. "Jeff's *your* mommy's old friend."

"I know."

"Maybe you'll all love each other and get married and you can live here and go to school with Roberta and me."

Ashley put down her empty glass. "I don't want my mommy to get married."

Help. "I'm not getting married, honey!" Gabi declared.

"Not even to Greg?"

"No!"

"I'm glad." That was no news to Gabi. Ashley had difficulty sharing her with anyone.

"Who's Greg?" Nicky interjected calmly.

"A man at my mom's school district."

Nicky looked at Gabi with innocent hazel eyes. "I bet Jeff's a lot nicer than Greg, and he's a ranger like my dad!"

"Jeff's very nice," Gabi agreed, trying not to smile. The understatement of the century.

"Dad says Jeff needs a wife instead of all those girl-friends, then he won't be so restless. It'll make him an even better ranger."

Gabi couldn't decide whether to laugh or cry. What she did know was that this conversation had to end.

"I have a great idea. We'll go for a walk and buy some ice cream at Curry Village, but before we go I have to clean up the kitchen. While I'm doing that, why don't you call your mother, Nicky? We have to make sure it's all right with her."

"Okay."

"Here's the phone." She handed him the cordless. Ridiculous as it was, Nicky's comments mouthed by his father let her know Jeff's social life wasn't suffering. Surely she couldn't be jealous after all this time.

Chapter Four

"Ranger Sims is on line one for you, Jeff."

"Thanks, Diane."

It was ten to three. Knowing Gabi was at his house, Jeff couldn't concentrate on his work any longer and was ready to leave the office. But he had to take this call. After emailing instructions to the plumbing crew installing some new latrines at Hodgdon Meadow, he picked up. "Mark? What's happening?"

"Can I ask you something?"

Jeff grunted. "What kind of a question is that?"

"Maybe I misunderstood about you keeping Sergei with you while Cal's away on his honeymoon."

"No. I've got him."

"Did you hire a dog handler to babysit him while you're at work? Whoever she is has caught the eye of a half-dozen rangers here in the village." Jeff shot out of his chair. "The calls have been coming in about this gorgeous female with black hair attached to Cal's dog. I thought I'd better check on it."

"That woman is an old family friend of mine who's just passing through the park."

"Every ranger should have *that* kind of an old friend."

"It isn't what you're thinking, Mark. She's with her daughter. I guess they decided to take Sergei for a walk until I got off work."

"Whatever you say."

Jeff was trying to see the humor in it. "Did any of those Peeping Toms mention Nicky was with her?"

"Not that I recall. This wouldn't be the woman Ranger Finlay was checking on for you yesterday, would it? He said you burst into the office like you were on the verge of having a heart attack. Now that he's seen her, he can understand why."

Damn. "Tell the guys to calm down."

"That's kind of hard to do now that the beautiful filly is out of the barn, so to speak. Finlay did a little detective work and found out she's staying at the Yosemite Lodge tonight."

That was news to Jeff. Gabi had gotten busy while he'd been at work.

"Does that mean you wouldn't be averse to Ranger Finlay or Ranger Ness, who saw her first, dropping in on her at the lodge this evening for a friendly visit?"

"This doesn't have anything to do with me, but you should know she's just come out of a divorce and needs peace of mind for a little while."

"I was only doing what the guys asked me to do. Now that you've explained, I'll let everyone know she's off-limits, without giving anything away."

"I'd appreciate that."

"How long have you been friends?"

"Since I was fifteen."

Mark whistled.

"Our families lived next door to each other in Alhambra. She's having trouble with her ex-husband and wanted a few days off from worry." If the time came that Jeff needed extra security for her while she was here, Mark would be the man to call on for help.

"Is he stalking her?"

Jeff decided to be honest with him, and told him what he knew.

"If the man's been in the military, then that adds an extra layer of complication, for several reasons," Mark theorized. "Why don't you let me cancel the lodge reservation."

"You're reading my mind. While you're at it, erase her from the system. She'll be staying with me."

"I'll get right on it and spread the word that any info about her is classified."

"Thanks, Mark. For now, she's waiting on the advice of her attorney."

"Yeah, well, we all know that an abusive ex-husband who has seen action and is upset knows no boundaries. He'll ignore a gag or restraining order without giving it a thought." Jeff's thoughts exactly. "Keep in touch."

"Will do."

Relieved to have an ally, he hung up and left headquarters before anything else could prevent him from getting out of there. On the way home he stopped for groceries. With that taken care of, he was halfway down the street to his house when he caught sight of three heads. Two with black hair, one with blond.

Nicky and Ashley were holding the dogs' leashes. Gabi walked behind them. Given her coloring and looks, he couldn't blame the other guys for staring. Having a baby had filled out her figure. The shape of her head, the enticing Gypsy hairstyle... She had everything feminine that called out to a man.

Seeing her here was still hard to believe. Though he wished she'd come for a different reason, he wasn't going to complain. Catching up with her again would allow him to explain a few things. Forced to leave Alhambra the way he did had torn him up inside. If nothing else, he wanted her to know why there'd been no time to talk.

"There's Jeff!" he heard Nicky cry as he pulled in the driveway. Jeff jumped down from the cab and walked toward them. Sergei saw him and lunged forward, causing the leash to pull away from Ashley.

"Hey, buddy!" He hunkered down to hug him. "Have you been a good boy for her?" He looked up into the adorable face that reminded him so much of her mother.

"He obeyed me all the time until just now."

Jeff smiled at her. "I'm glad to hear it. Sounds like you did a great job of taking care of him." He pulled out his wallet and gave her a ten-dollar bill. "That's for being such a good dog walker. This ought to pay for a Yosemite Sam T-shirt."

"They're cool!" Nicky interjected.

"Thanks!" The cute little pixie put it in her jeans pocket. "We're glad you came home."

His gaze flicked to Gabi, who was staring down at him with the kind of soft expression in those periwinkle eyes he remembered. "It's nice to know someone around here missed me," he murmured.

"You were at work!" Nicky reminded him. "Aren't you still supposed to be there?"

Nicky, Nicky. The boy was sounding more and more like the chief every day. "I thought I'd get started fixing dinner for us."

"You must be hungry to come home this early."

You don't know the half of it, sport. "Yup."

"Are we going to have hot dogs?"

"Nope. Tortilla pie with guacamole."

"What's that?"

"Gabi will tell you." He liked being able to put her on the spot.

"What is it, Mommy?"

"It's like tacos, but you make it like a pie with lots of cheese. Jeff's mother used to fix it all the time."

"Did you like it?" Ashley asked her.

"I loved it," she muttered. "Come on, everyone. Let's go in the house. The dogs need a drink."

Jeff got to his feet. "Nicky? You know where the checkers are. While I freshen up, why don't you start a game with Ashley in the living room?"

"Okay. I brought Match-Up, too. We can play it when we get tired."

"I play that with Jessica," Ashley informed him.

"Who's Jessica?"

"My best friend. She lives across the street from me. I win at that game more than she does."

"So do I. My dad says I'm hard to beat."

Gabi's eyes met Jeff's. Their laughter would be heard all over the park if they dared let it out.

He went inside ahead of them. Sergei went straight to the kitchen, and a few minutes later reentered the living room and lay on the floor next to the kids, who'd started their checkers game.

Jeff found Gabi in the kitchen. "I don't see your suitcases anywhere."

She rubbed the palms of her hands against her jean-clad hips, drawing his attention to them. "I put them back in the car. Now that we're alone I wanted to tell you I've made a reservation at the Yosemite Lodge for tonight. Ashley and I will leave after we've eaten."

Jeff got started on their dinner. She helped him, just like old times. They worked in harmony. "I'm afraid your reservation has been cancelled by the chief of park security."

Color filled her cheeks. "I wish you hadn't asked him to do that, Jeff. Don't you understand I don't want to impose on you?"

"How could you possibly be imposing when I'm the one who followed you to El Portal?" He started browning the ground beef for the pie. "I told him about your situation and he agreed that should your ex-husband get desperate, he'll go to any lengths to find you.

"I doubt he'd be able to trace you here, but to be on the safe side your name has been erased from the park's system. We can't do anything about your stay at the Travelodge last night."

If the redhead at the front desk was given the chance, she'd probably tell all if Gabi's ex were to show up asking questions. Jeff would worry about that remote possibility at a later date.

Gabi shook her dark head. "Jeff—"

"It's settled," he insisted. "There's a cot in the guest

bedroom and the couch turns into a pullout bed, so the sleeping arrangements are all taken care of."

"I should never have come," she whispered.

He put the pie in the oven before opening the fridge to pull out the ingredients for a green salad. "I'm glad you did. We have unfinished business between us."

With her head still averted, she said, "I don't know what you mean."

"What, exactly, did your foster mother tell you after you found out I'd left Alhambra?"

The silence lasted so long, he wondered if she'd even heard him. "Gabi?" he prodded.

"She said you'd decided to go away to college."

"That was it?"

"Yes."

He made a sound in his throat. "Did you ask my dad?"

"When I saw his truck pull in the driveway the next evening, I went over to your house to talk to him. Ellen answered the door and told me you'd moved out. I asked her where you'd gone. She said that if you wanted me to know, you'd get in touch with me. When she shut the door in my face without telling your father I'd come over, I got the message and never went back."

Jeff had to tamp down his anger. There were too many truths Gabi didn't know anything about yet, but now wasn't the time to divulge Bev's role in the story. For the moment Bev was Gabi's friend, not the enemy. He would allow Gabi to go on believing that until a later time, when the danger from her ex was over. But he could be honest about his father's part in what had happened.

"My dad could see how close we were getting, Gabi. He was afraid my interest in you would prevent me from going away to college. To be blunt, he feared I might get you pregnant. Ellen backed him up and added that it would be considered statutory rape, because you were only seventeen."

"That's true." She grabbed a knife and started chopping onions for the salad. "Bev gave me and Nora several lectures on the same subject before Nora turned eighteen and left Alhambra, after you did."

Jeff just bet Bev had. "I told my dad we hadn't slept together, but he warned me it would only be a matter of time." His father had been right about that.

"I told Bev we hadn't done anything wrong," Gabi said, "but I don't think she believed me. Now that I'm older, I can see why she was worried. We spent too much time together."

"They were all worried about us," he admitted. "Dad finally convinced me you were too young for me, and needed the chance to get through the rest of high school without me being around. But it wasn't until he brought up your past that I made the decision to go."

"*My* past?"

"Yes. He asked me if I wanted history to repeat itself where you were concerned. When I asked him what he meant, he said that your birth mother and father were probably underage and that's why you'd been abandoned after you were born."

She froze, then glanced at Jeff. "You and I already had that discussion and came to the same conclusion."

"Yup. There wasn't anything Dad said that you and I hadn't already thought or talked about." Jeff finished slicing the tomatoes and put them in the salad bowl. "After he ended his lecture, I told him I would move out. Ellen was thrilled to see the back of me and couldn't get rid of me fast enough."

Ellen had said a lot of things to Jeff in private, claiming that Gabi was nothing more than trash coming up through the government system. That he could do much better for himself once he got out in the world.

"I think she was jealous of your mother's memory."

He nodded. "She wanted Dad to herself, but soon found out Mom was impossible to replace."

"I loved Ruth," Gabi whispered.

"So did I."

"Her death changed your father. So did his second marriage."

"Life was never the same after that," Jeff agreed. "Dad was continually on my case. He made me promise I wouldn't phone or write you. 'A clean break,' he said. 'No goodbyes. Just leave and give Gabi time to grow up first, son. Then if she's still around and you're still interested…'"

"I see," Gabi said in a tremulous voice.

"So I took off, determined to make some good money and start college, to give you space. The week after you turned eighteen, I came back to Alhambra to bring you a birthday present and talk to you, but Bev told me you'd moved out."

Gabi gasped quietly and lifted her head. "You came to the house?" He nodded. "She never said a word."

"That doesn't surprise me. I asked her for a forwarding address or phone number, but she said she couldn't give it to me without your permission."

A pained expression crossed Gabi's face. "That's true. You left in June. I waited the whole month to hear from you. When July came and you still hadn't come home or phoned or sent me a letter, I told Bev that if you ever tried to contact me, she was to say I didn't want to see or talk to you again. But that didn't mean—" She stopped midsentence. "Oh, well, it doesn't matter. "

He grimaced. Bev had gotten her wish, and had definitely enjoyed telling him Gabi was better off without him. "After leaving the way I did the first time, without saying goodbye to you, I deserved that, Gabi."

"Where were you living by then?"

"In Culver City." At the revelation her eyes dimmed. "I asked around the neighborhood about you. No one knew where you'd gone. Before I drove back home, I went by Kim's house, hoping she might give me some information about you. To my surprise, her family had moved. Someone else lived there and didn't know anything."

"Her father got a job in Portland." Gabi's color had faded. "Excuse me for a minute." She left the kitchen.

Alarmed, Jeff followed her down the hall, where she hurried into the guest bathroom and shut the door. Unfortunately, Ashley saw her.

"Mommy?" she called out in a panic, running toward the bathroom.

"It's okay, honey." Jeff rushed to pick her up. "Your mom just got a nosebleed," he lied without compunction. "She'll be out in a minute."

"My mom got a lot of them before Parker was born," Nicky informed her. "Is your mom going to have a baby?"

GABI CLUNG TO the bathroom sink for a minute in order to deal with Jeff's stunning revelations. He'd left home because of Mr. Thompson? She'd always thought Jeff's father liked her. She couldn't take it in.

When Jeff had come by the house a year later, it was her own fault Bev hadn't given him any information. Yet in all the years since the divorce, her foster mother hadn't once mentioned anything about that incident. Surely it would have been the kind thing for Bev to do. She'd known how much Gabi had suffered through her last year of high school because Jeff had gone away.

The face staring at her in the mirror looked pale. She leaned over and washed it with warm water, then put on fresh lipstick. When she'd gotten her nerves under some semblance of control, she left the bathroom and walked into the living room, where everyone had congregated.

"Mommy?" Ashley ran over to her. Sergei followed her. "Are you going to have a baby?" she whispered.

Gabi blinked. "Where on earth would you get an idea like that?"

"Because Jeff said you had a nosebleed."

That was quick thinking. "I did have one, but it's gone now and I'm all better. Why do you think that means I'm going to have a baby?"

"Because Nicky's mom got them before her baby was born."

"Ah." Gabi hugged her daughter before addressing her and Nicky. "People get nosebleeds for all kinds of reasons, but I'm not going to have a baby. I bumped my nose on the kitchen door by accident."

Jeff shot her a smiling glance. "I did the same thing

the other day. Maybe I should take it off the hinges. Come on. Dinner's ready. We'll eat in the dining room. Everyone can help."

Before long the four of them were seated around the table. The dogs had assembled, hoping for any crumb that dropped. Gabi had no appetite, but she needed to pretend for her daughter's sake. And Jeff's.

Everything he'd told her in the kitchen had come as a shock, and he knew it. But she didn't want him reading anything significant into it. Theirs was a past history, better forgotten now that she knew the truth. As he'd said earlier in the day, she looked as if she could use a friend. Until she and Ashley left tomorrow, she could pretend, and do the old-friend thing.

When there was a knock on the front door, Jeff got up from the table and disappeared into the other room. In a second Gabi heard another deep male voice. Nicky heard it, too. "That's my dad. Hey, Dad—we're in here!"

Two attractive men entered the dining room. The chief ranger wasn't the boy's biological father. He had dark hair and wore a broad smile. "Hi, sport!"

"Hi! We're eating tortilla pie. It's pretty good!"

The grown-ups chuckled, and Jeff introduced everyone. "Chief Rossiter, this is Ashley Rafferty and her mother, Gabi, an old friend of mine from Rosemead."

He shook their hands. "Welcome to Yosemite. What do you think of the park so far, Ashley?"

"I like it, but how come there's no water at Yosemite Falls?"

He smiled. "August is the month it's mostly a trickle, but later on, with more rainfall, the water will start to cascade down again. Spring is when the views are most spectacular and Yosemite Falls is at its mightiest."

Jeff nodded. "If you want to see a beautiful waterfall now, I'll take you to Bridalveil Falls in the morning. I have to go up there early for an inspection."

"It's an easy hike," Nicky interjected. "The water falls six hundred feet."

Ashley looked excited. "That's a lot, huh."

"Yup."

"Can Sergei come?"

"He wouldn't miss it," Jeff proclaimed.

Nicky glanced at his dad. "Can I go, too?"

"If it's all right with Jeff."

"The more, the merrier."

"I wish I had a dog like him," Ashley said with a sigh.

"He's a real hit around here," the chief stated.

Jeff pulled out another chair. "You're welcome to eat with us."

"I'd love to, but it will have to be another time. Rachel's parents arrived at the house a little while ago for dinner, and she's expecting us home now. Let's go, sport, and don't tell your mom you've already eaten. Be sure and thank Jeff."

"Okay." Nicky slid off the chair. "Thanks for everything, Jeff."

"You're welcome here anytime."

The darling boy looked at Ashley. "Do you want to play after our hike?" She nodded. "Then you can keep the games and binoculars until tomorrow."

"Thanks."

"Be really careful with them. Dad gave them to me for a special present."

"I wish I had binoculars like yours. I promise I won't hurt them. Maybe I'll be able to see that woodpecker before I go to bed."

"Jeff will show you."

"Sure I will." He ruffled Nicky's blond hair with affection.

Gabi decided not to say anything. Except for being Jeff's houseguest for tonight, she didn't know the rest of her plans. Tomorrow, after the hike, they'd leave the park, but now wasn't the time to discuss it.

Chief Rossiter nodded to her and Ashley. "We'll see you tomorrow. Good night."

While everyone else walked to the front door, Gabi got busy clearing the table. Her daughter soon returned to help her. Jeff joined them while they were loading the dishwasher.

"Where would you like to sleep tonight, Ashley?"

"With my mom."

He flicked Gabi a glance. "Then you two can sleep in my bed and I'll sleep in the guest room."

Gabi bit her lip. "But there's only a cot."

"That's fine with me. Since I became a ranger, I've probably slept on more cots than beds. While you finish up here, I'll put on clean sheets." He took off before she could argue.

The best solution would be to let Ashley sleep with her tonight, Gabi decided. They were both exhausted and there'd be no histrionics. Tomorrow she'd leave the park and find another place to hide out for a time. No matter what, she couldn't continue to stay with Jeff.

By the time the kitchen was clean, Jeff's bedroom was ready for them. He'd already put their suitcases inside. Fresh towels sat on the bed. "When we get back, you can bathe or shower in my bathroom. I'll use the one down the hall," he told them.

"Where are we going?"

Jeff flashed Ashley an intriguing smile. "If you're not too tired, I thought maybe you and your mom would like to walk over to Curry Village to hear a program about the park. We'll take Sergei with us."

Ashley's head jerked to Gabi with excitement. "Could we, Mom?" Obviously, there was no sign of fatigue from her daughter.

"That sounds fun."

"We'll have to leave now if we don't want to miss the storytelling."

"I'm ready!"

"So is Sergei." Jeff grinned. "He's waiting for you to lead him. Here. You can put on his leash."

"Come on, Sergei." By now Ashley was so natural with the dog, it seemed they belonged together. Amazing!

Gabi glanced at Jeff. "Give me one second." Her purse was on the bed. She reached for it and hurried into the bathroom to run a brush through her hair and put on lipstick.

Before long they left the house and walked through the complex to the amphitheater. The temperature had to be in the seventies. Perfect weather. She felt as if they were a normal married couple out for a twilight stroll with the family. The whole effect was surreal, because in her girlhood dreams she'd fantasized about her and

Jeff doing this very kind of thing one day, with their own children and a mutt like Nicky's.

Of course, at seventeen Gabi had never heard of a Karelian bear dog, nor had she imagined Yosemite as the backdrop in her dreams. While her mind was caught up in past musings, her daughter was being besieged by tourists who recognized Sergei from the news. When the attention grew too much, Jeff had to take over.

With the program about ready to start, Gabi discovered many eyes focused on them. The tourists could be forgiven for staring at Sergei. But Gabi knew deep down it was an excuse for the females in the audience to check out the rugged-looking ranger whose hard-muscled body was pressed against her side. The large crowd meant they'd all had to squeeze together.

It reminded her of the hundreds of times she'd gone for rides on the back of Jeff's motorcycle after school and on weekends. Rides giving them freedom to go wherever they wanted in order to have privacy. He'd tell her to put her arms around him and hold on tight. As if she'd needed any urging. She would have ridden off into the sunrise, sunset or any time in between with him, never to return, if he'd suggested it.

By the time he found seats for them and the speaker took the stage, Gabi came back out of her reverie.

"Welcome to the soundscape show. Sounds alert you to the things you've come to see at Yosemite," the presenter began. "Close your eyes and listen very intently to every sound you hear in the park. A bird's warble, running water, wind whistling around the granite structures—all of these take on new meaning because the acoustical depth here is much greater than in the city.

"Turn off the sound in a movie, and the quality of the experience decreases. But the opposite happens when you enter Yosemite and leave the noise behind. You see, man-made sounds interfere with the beautiful sounds of nature. Periodic immersion in quiet park landscapes are beneficial to humans and wildlife alike, affecting the internal ecosystem.

"Listen to this bleet of a bighorn sheep. Now listen to this juvenile bear being driven off by its mom for annoying her. Those are sounds natural in the park setting, but most of us will never hear them because of human engines. When you get up in Yosemite's back country, there are intervals between jets flying over where it's one of the quietest places in the U.S. That's when you'll hear nature at her best."

The program fascinated Gabi. But by the time it was over and the crowd started to disburse, she could see Ashley's eyelids drooping. "Let's get you home to bed, honey."

Sergei led the way, pulling Ashley along. Jeff put a hand on her shoulder. "Which part of the presentation did you like the best?"

"The sound of the baby bear getting mad. That was funny," she said with a giggle.

Jeff slanted his gaze to Gabi. "What about you?"

"I loved all of it. Too bad the explorer John Muir couldn't have recorded the accidental sounds of the park back then when there was much less man-made noise."

Ashley looked up at Jeff. "Does that woodpecker make sounds?"

"Tell you what—the binoculars won't do us much

good now that it's dark, but as soon as we get back, we'll sneak up close to the tree and stand very still. Maybe we'll hear him."

One of the things Gabi had loved about Jeff was his sense of adventure. He also possessed a manliness that had stood out from the other guys she'd known at school. Even as a teen she'd felt perfectly safe with him in any situation. Gabi realized he was still the most exciting male she'd ever met or known.

"We're almost to the house," he whispered to Ashley. "Let me hold you and Sergei. From here on, no one says a word." He picked Ashley up and held her in one arm while he guided the dog with the other. Together the four of them moved closer to the tree in question.

Watching him with Ashley reminded Gabi of a time when she and Jeff had been enjoying a picnic at the park, and a flock of European starlings had descended. Suddenly there were thousands of black birds swarming all around them, foraging for food. She'd never seen a sight like it. Jeff had sensed her fear and pulled her close, telling her not to be nervous. His words and the feel of his arms around her had dispelled her anxiety.

The memory of that incident sent a little thrill through her body as she saw how Ashley held on to him without being the least bit hesitant or shy. He had a way with people that instilled confidence.

Jeff led them to within a few feet of the tree. While Ashley looked up, his gaze met Gabi's, and her breath caught. In the quiet of the night they heard distinct tapping.

Ashley forgot not to talk. "There he is! It sounds like he's knocking on the door."

"Yup," Jeff responded. "His own little house in the forest."

She giggled. "You're funny." They listened some more. The moment was magical. "Uh-oh. He stopped pecking."

"He'll be back after we go in the house." They headed for the front porch.

"Has Nicky heard him pecking?"

"I'm not sure."

"Do you think he could sleep over tomorrow night so he could hear him pecking, too?"

"Tomorrow we'll ask his mom. If she says yes, then he can sleep on the pullout couch with Samson."

"Thanks, Jeff." Ashley kissed him on the cheek before he put her down to unlock the door.

Gabi had gone out with several men over the past school year, men who'd been good to her daughter. But she'd never seen Ashley come close to kissing any man of her acquaintance, not even Greg, who'd gone out of his way to make dinner special for them last week.

More than ever they needed to leave tomorrow. Ashley wouldn't like it, but there was no other option. Gabi didn't want her daughter to get too attached to Jeff. Already it was happening. Just now she'd given her affection to him so freely, it reminded Gabi of herself when she'd discovered the wonderful older boy next door. *Like mother, like daughter?*

"Come on, honey. Tell Jeff thank-you, then let's get those teeth brushed."

"Okay." She gave Sergei a hug, then looked up at Jeff. "I really liked the program."

He tousled her dark curls. "So did I. It's fun when you can see it with friends."

"Could Sergei sleep with Mommy and me?"

"No, Ashley," Gabi declared in a firm tone, staring directly at Jeff as she spoke. "Jeff is taking care of the dog for his best friend and has certain rules for him. Good night, Jeff. We owe you a debt of gratitude for what you've done for us, and we won't forget." She bent over to pet the dog. "Good night, Sergei."

Grasping her daughter's hand, she walked her down the hall to the bedroom.

"Get a good sleep, Ashley. Don't let the bedbugs bite," Jeff teased from the other end of the house.

She turned around with a smile. "Don't let the woodpecker peck you."

With that clever, unexpected retort, both Gabi and Jeff broke into laughter. When it subsided he murmured something about Nicky having met his match.

"What did he say?" Ashley asked after they'd gone in the bedroom.

"I didn't quite hear him," Gabi replied.

"He's nice, Mommy."

She opened Ashley's suitcase to get out her pajamas. "You think?"

"I like him better than Greg."

"I can understand that. He let you play with Sergei. That was very nice of him, considering Sergei's such an important dog."

"Nicky told me Ranger Davis really likes him."

"Who? The dog?"

"No." Ashley let out a little trill of laughter. "Jeff!"

She knew exactly who her daughter meant. Jeff had

mentioned a Ranger Davis the other day, but at the time Gabi hadn't realized it was a female colleague. Though she hated asking the next question, she couldn't help herself. "How does Nicky know something like that?"

"He heard his mommy talking to her at the pool on her day off from work."

That Nicky. "He shouldn't listen in on other people's conversations." Gabi had a feeling the cute little rascal did a lot of that. She was about to tell her daughter not to listen to any more of his secrets, but refrained, because tomorrow they'd be leaving Yosemite and wouldn't be back. It made any warning unnecessary.

"Let's say our prayers, then it's lights out."

Chapter Five

Ashley looked up at Jeff once they'd made the twenty-minute climb from the trailhead. "It's really pretty, but I don't think it looks like a bridal veil."

"I don't, either," Nicky chimed in.

"That's because there isn't much water right now. In the spring, when it's gushing, the breeze blows the mist and makes it look like a veil draped over a bride's face," Jeff explained.

This was one of the most glorious views in Yosemite, but all he could see was the breathtaking woman dressed in jeans and a summery yellow top, taking in the sights. The morning light glinted in her dark, curly hair. He could well imagine sheer, white lace covering Gabi's beautiful features.

Jeff could envision himself lifting that veil to kiss the luscious red mouth beneath. All night long those lips had haunted him, bringing back memories of the passion they'd once shared. Though they'd been teenagers, their feelings had been real, and had run deep.

Whatever history had gone on for her since then, she'd come here after seeing his picture. That she'd instinctively sought him out was something to cherish, at least.

"My mom wore a veil when she got married, didn't you, Mommy?"

"Yes," Gabi answered faintly. She had been quiet all morning, no doubt trying to control her fears over what her ex-husband was up to right now.

"So did mine." Nicky piped up. "It was really long and Uncle Chase let out a big cough because Dad couldn't find the end of it."

Gabi's amused eyes met Jeff's, and for an instant he caught the flecks of purple in them. His heartbeat sped up before she glanced away again. He remembered the countless times they'd looked at each other like that, totally keyed in to what the other was thinking.

Much as he wanted to have one of their old talks, he couldn't do it here in front of the children, or the tourists who'd spotted Sergei and started crowding around.

"I'd better take over with the dog till we reach the Volvo, Ashley."

"Okay." She handed him the leash.

"What do you guys say we head back to the Pizza Patio for lunch before I have to put in a few hours work?"

"Hooray!" Nicky cried.

When Jeff reached his office, there'd be a bunch of reports to get through. Mondays tended to start off hectic, but for once he'd had something important and personal to do this morning, and had asked Diane to cover for him. If there'd been an emergency, she would have phoned him.

"You'll like the pizza," Nicky confided to Ashley

during the easy descent to the parking lot. "I like pepperoni."

"So do I, but I don't like onions."

"I like those, but I don't like mushrooms or peppers."

The cute little kids had no problem communicating. The problem was Gabi, who hadn't said more than a couple words since getting up this morning. She walked next to him, with their arms and hips occasionally brushing because of all the people on the trail. With every step, Jeff's awareness of her grew, swamping him with wants that had lain dormant for years. But he knew her thoughts were concentrated on her ex-husband.

He had to be all kinds of a fool to be caught up in his own desires when she was on a nightmarish countdown before facing Ashley's father. The thought of her former husband physically abusing her or Ashley because he couldn't have what he wanted gutted Jeff.

When they reached the car, Sergei climbed in back with the kids. Jeff helped Gabi in, then they took off for Curry Village. En route he gave her a covert glance, marveling over the phenomenal success she'd made of her life.

She'd come into this world destined to be an orphan, and had lived in a succession of foster homes without the support of a loving mother and father. Yet she'd held jobs, managed to study and get a college degree and teach school, all the while being a superb mother to Ashley. He couldn't praise her enough for what she'd accomplished. For her ex-husband to explode back in her life like this wasn't fair.

But then, nothing was fair. His hands tightened on

the steering wheel. Jeff's own mom had died too young, forcing him to accept Ellen, the virtual wicked step-mother replacement. Between her machinations, which had held his dad hostage, and Bev White's agenda, which had involved Nora's willing cooperation, Jeff had been left with no choice but to leave Gabi strictly alone, or else...

If life could have gone on and played out normally over the next couple of years, with no evil subplots to sabotage his plans, Gabi would have ended up being Jeff's wife. He was positive of it! By now they might have produced a child like Ashley. She was as precious as Nicky.

Jeff could see why Chief Rossiter's heart had been touched by the little boy who'd lost his parents on top of El Capitan. When Vance had fallen in love with Rachel, that love had included her nephew. Already Jeff could feel his own heart responding to Gabi's daughter. The fierce need to protect both of them had taken hold.

"Has everyone finished eating?"

Gabi flashed him a glance. "I know you need to get to work. Why don't you leave now? The children and I will get ice cream and walk home."

"Tell you what. I'll give you the car key so you can drive home when you're ready." He drew the key chain from his pocket and pulled off the one in question, hand-ing it to her. "The remote for the garage is on the visor. The door into the kitchen is unlocked. Since Samson isn't with you, I'll take Sergei with me. That will free you up to do whatever you want this afternoon."

Her blue eyes stared into his. "Thank you for a won-derful morning."

"The pleasure was all mine." She had no idea. After getting to his feet, he put a couple of bills on the table to pay for their meal. "See you guys in a while."

Ashley waved. "Bye, Jeff. Hurry back. We have more fun with you."

Is that so? Did you hear that, Gabi?

"See ya later, alligator!" Nicky blurted his trademark response. On cue, Gabi's lips curved into a smile.

It took a lot of self-control not to hug her. Instead Jeff patted two heads and took off with Sergei. The sooner he got his work done, the sooner he could get back to them. Later on, when Ashley went to bed, he'd get Gabi alone in the living room where they could really talk.

AN HOUR LATER, Gabi was watching the kids playing outside from the living-room window when her phone rang. She checked the caller ID and picked up immediately.

"Hello?"

"Mrs. Rafferty?"

"Yes?"

"I'm Janine, Mr. Steel's paralegal. We're both at the courthouse right now. He's in a trial that will last all day, so he asked me to phone you. Could you be at his office tomorrow at ten in the morning? There've been some new developments in your case he needs to discuss with you."

New developments? Panic brought her to her feet. "Could you tell me what they are?"

"I'm sorry, but I'm not at liberty to talk about your case."

"No, of course not." But it didn't sound good.

"Can I tell him you'll be there?'

"Yes." Gabi would have to bring Ashley with her and leave her in the reception room while the meeting took place. "Thank you for calling."

Mr. Steel's office was near the corner of Sunset and Doheny in Los Angeles. After she hung up, she phoned several different motel chains until she found one in the area. Once she'd made a reservation for tonight—indicating they would probably arrive late—she clicked off and started packing their things.

Depending on what she learned in that meeting, she would know if it was safe to go back to their apartment in Rosemead. If not, she'd figure out something else. Jeff's intervention had given her time to get her head on straight, but she refused to impose on his generosity another night.

The children were still outside, looking through the binoculars. It gave her time to change the sheets and write Jeff a thank-you note, which she put on the kitchen counter along with his car key and fifty dollars cash. If she gave him any more money, he wouldn't like it.

Without the children being aware, she carried the suitcases out to her car, parked in the garage next to the Volvo. After gathering up Nicky's games, she put them in the car and backed out of the garage next to the truck parked in the driveway. Going back inside, she shut the garage door, then left the house through the front door and locked it.

The children ran up to her. "Where are we going, Mommy?" her daughter cried.

"We have some things to do right now, honey, so we'll run Nicky home."

Ashley frowned. "Can't he come with us?"

"I think his mom needs him to help her, and he has to take care of Samson. Shall we go?"

They climbed in the back. "Can he come over again later?" Ashley asked.

"We'll see."

"Okay."

Gabi backed out to the street. "I've never been to your house, Nicky. Will you tell me where to go?"

"Sure." Following his directions, Gabi drove down two streets, turned right and stopped where he told her.

"Don't forget your games and binoculars."

"I won't."

"We'll wait here until you're safely inside."

He nodded, not at all happy. Neither was her daughter.

"Bye, Nicky," Ashley said quietly.

"Bye." He scrambled out of the car with his things and hurried into his house. Pretty soon his mother appeared at the door holding her baby. She was blonde like Nicky. "Thank you for bringing him home! I was just about to phone you," she called.

"Thank *you* for letting him play with Ashley. We'll have to do it again."

"Absolutely. Next time, your daughter can come over here."

"I'm sure she'd love that. Goodbye."

Quiet reigned until they reached the next corner, then Ashley said, "Why couldn't I go in his house and play?"

Here came the hard part. "Because something important has come up and we have to drive back to Los Angeles today."

"But I want to stay here. Jeff's coming home later."

"I know, but we have to go."

She burst into tears. "Jeff said we were going to do something fun after he got home from work. Sergei was going to come with us."

"I'm sorry, honey, but while you were outside with Nicky, I received a phone call about an important meeting I have to attend in the morning. That's why we have to get back."

"Couldn't I stay with Jeff? He'd let me. He told me he likes me a lot. I'd be good."

Already he'd built such confidence in her, Ashley was a different child.

"Of course you would, and Jeff has been wonderful to both of us. But you have to remember he's the chief steward of the park, with huge responsibilities. You couldn't stay alone with him. If there was an emergency, he and Sergei would have to leave the house to join the other rangers, and there'd be no one to look after you."

"Nicky's mom would tend me."

Good heavens. "You haven't even met her, honey. Even if she would let you stay, our vacation is over." Being with Jeff again had been a gift Gabi would cherish forever, but to stay any longer wasn't possible, not with tomorrow's meeting looming.

Gabi decided the phone call from the paralegal had come at a fortuitous moment. After watching Ashley around Jeff, it was clear she was starved for a daddy's attention and would take all the affection Jeff was prepared to shower on her. What her daughter didn't understand was that he was a bachelor who, except for this chance encounter, was out of reach of their world, both physically and emotionally.

The irony didn't escape Gabi that Ashley's biological father had shown up again like some frightening phantom who could slip past any defense because he had DNA rights.

Gabi drew in a fortifying breath. The talk she needed to have with Ashley about her father was almost upon them. Her little girl would have dozens of questions. After tomorrow's meeting, Gabi would know how to answer them, no matter how painful. But she dreaded tomorrow because their beautiful world was going to change.

"Honey? At the first town outside the park we'll buy you some art supplies so you can draw in the car."

"I don't want to draw," Ashley said with tears in her voice.

"Think how fun it would be for Nicky if he got a few pictures you'd made for him. You're a terrific artist. He'd love it if you drew Samson and Sergei. We could send them to his daddy at park headquarters and he'd make sure Nicky got them."

"I'll do a woodpecker for Jeff!"

Jeff again. "He'll love it!"

After another minute Ashley asked, "Does he know we left?"

"Not yet, but I wrote him a letter and thanked him for everything. He'll see it when he gets home."

"Sergei will look for me."

"I'm sure he will, but remember something. He's a

bear dog and has been missing his real master. Ranger
Hollis will be coming back to the park at the end of the
week. Think how happy Sergei will be."

"Then Jeff will be all alone," Ashley said in a forlorn
voice.

"Honey—he *likes* being alone."

"Is that why he got divorced?"

"I have no idea what happened."

Gabi could hear the wheels turning. "Do *you* like
being alone, Mommy?"

"I'm not alone. I have you. You're the light of my
life. I love you, darling girl."

She heard a sniff. "I love you, too."

JEFF WAS ABOUT TO PHONE Gabi and let her know he
was coming home when he heard Nicky's voice drift-
ing from Diane's office. Sergei had already jumped to
his feet.

No doubt Nicky was giving Ashley the grand tour of
the place, as only he could do. With a smile, Jeff started
to push himself away from his desk, eager to see the
kids, but Nicky walked in alone. Sergei greeted him,
rubbing his head against his legs.

Everyone loved the chief's son. He was unique and
funny and happy, which was why Jeff hardly recognized
the downcast look on his cute face. "Hey, Nicky—why
is my favorite junior ranger looking so glum? I thought
you were playing with Ashley."

"We were until her mom drove me home. I thought
maybe they were here with you, but Diane said she
hadn't seen them."

Uh-oh. "Why did Gabi do that? Did you and Ashley have an argument?"

"No. We were outside watching for the woodpecker with my binoculars when Ashley's mom backed their car out of the garage and told us to get in because she had things to do."

Jeff's brows furrowed. "That was all she said?"

The boy nodded. "Mom said Ashley could sleep over at my house tonight and maybe Roberta would come, too. Dad wants to have a barbecue."

"That sounds fun." In fact, the plans couldn't be more tailor-made, so Jeff could have private time with Gabi. "They're probably shopping."

"Could you find out?" The boy's solemn eyes implored him.

"Sure." Jeff needed no urging. He reached for the phone and pressed the digits to call her number. To his frustration, after two rings he was told to leave a message. "Hi, Gabi. It's Jeff. Give me a call when you can. We're invited over to Chief Rossiter's for a barbecue this evening."

When he hung up, Nicky said, "Thanks, Jeff. See ya tonight." He ran out of the office with his usual exuberance.

Unable to concentrate, Jeff left headquarters through the back door and sprinted home, with Sergei at his side. The workout provided a needed release of excess energy. He let them in through the front door and called out. No one answered.

Sergei went in search of his water bowl. Jeff tossed his hat on a chair and followed him into the kitchen. He was about to grab a soda from the fridge when his heart plunged to his feet. Beneath the key and some money, he saw a folded note, and grabbed for it.

Dear Jeff, you've been the most cordial host in the world. I'll never be able to thank you enough for showing me and Ashley such a wonderful time. While you were at work, Mr. Steel called and told me I needed to be in his office at ten tomorrow morning for a meeting. He indicated there were new developments in my case, but I don't know what they are. Since it's a long drive to Los Angeles, I decided to leave immediately. I washed the sheets, but didn't have time to stay and put them in the dryer.

Good old Jeff. You were there for me when I was a teenager. You were there for me when I needed a respite from my terror. I'll never forget. Bless you. Gabi.

Like air escaping a slit tire, he felt all the joy of being with her again rush out of him, leaving him bereft. The talk he'd wanted to have with her wasn't destined to materialize.

Still on duty in case of an emergency, he couldn't leave the park and go after her. He couldn't even have a couple of beers to dull the pain. Not knowing which foot to put in front of the other, he barely managed to make it to the laundry room between the kitchen and the garage. Sure enough, he found the sheets and pillowcases and put them in the dryer, then wandered through the house to his bedroom, Sergei following him.

She'd left it and the bathroom in perfect condition. Experiencing a different kind of grief than he'd known before, he stretched out on the bed with his hands behind his head and closed his eyes. A heavy sigh escaped.

Gabi, Gabi.

What was he going to do about her?

For years he'd fought the memory of the underage girl who'd claimed his heart long before he had the legal right to do anything about it. He'd gone through one woman after another, looking for fulfillment, until he'd heard she'd married. The pain had been too much and he'd made the mistake of marrying Fran on the rebound. Since his divorce, his relationships with women had been hollow.

Now, after appearing for an instant with her charming daughter, Gabi was gone again, to an uncertain future filled with fear, thrusting him down the same black hole he'd been trying to climb out of for years.

I can't go through this a second time.

I won't.

He rolled off the bed and got to his feet. Without hesitation, he pulled out his phone and called his boss. The assistant chief ranger answered on the third ring.

"Jeff? What's going on?"

"Something personal has come up and I need time off whenever it can be arranged."

"I'll cover for you, and you can take it now."

Chase was the best. Jeff's hand tightened on the phone. "You're sure?"

"You're the only ranger in the park who hasn't asked for a favor yet this season. I happen to know you wouldn't have phoned if this wasn't an emergency. How much time do you need?"

That was a good question. "I don't know. A few days." He'd insist on some plain talk with Gabi. Otherwise, his life didn't make sense.

"Then let's plan on you being back on duty Thursday morning. If you need more time, call me."

"I don't know how to thank you."

"Forget it. What will you do with Sergei?"

"I have a couple of rangers in mind."

"Drop him off at my house on your way out. Roberta will be thrilled to take care of him." Her beagle had died recently and everyone knew she was still mourning it. "Bring all the stuff he needs."

"I owe you, Chase."

"I'll remember that."

The minute they hung up, Jeff phoned the airport in Merced and booked a flight to L.A. He would leave the Volvo in the long-term parking. When he arrived in Los Angeles, he'd phone Gabi. If she didn't answer, he'd drive to Rosemead in a rental car.

In the event he couldn't find her there, he'd get a motel for the night and show up at her attorney's office in the morning. A divorce lawyer with the name Henry Steel shouldn't be too difficult to find in the L.A. area. Jeff planned to be in the reception room when Gabi got through with her meeting.

Once he'd thrown some clothes in a suitcase and locked up the house, he drove Sergei over to Chase's place with all the doggy paraphernalia and treats. Roberta had been alerted and was waiting for him, eager to take over Sergei's care. It was very touching how much all the children loved Cal's dog.

With that accomplished, Jeff left Yosemite Valley. Only one more phone call to make. He pressed the digit to the Rossiter household. Rachel answered.

"Hi, Jeff. Nicky's been waiting for you to call. How soon can Ashley come over?"

"I'm afraid there's been a change in plans. Gabi had to drive back to Los Angeles today for an important meeting tomorrow. They've already left."

"Oh, dear. Nicky's not going to be happy with that news. He really likes her."

"She likes him, too. Hopefully, they'll be back to the park soon." Jeff would do everything in his power to make it happen.

"When Vance gets home, he'll start up the grill. If anyone can help Nicky get over his disappointment, it's my husband."

"You're right. There's no one like the chief! Tell Nicky hi from me."

"I will. Thanks for calling, I think."

They both hung up.

Jeff didn't envy Rachel trying to placate Nicky. When that little guy cared about something or someone, he couldn't let it go. After meeting Vance, he'd wanted him to be his new daddy. His love for the chief ranger had been apparent for everyone to see. Fortunately for him, Vance loved him back.

Jeff could understand the chief's love for another man's child. At first sight Ashley had gotten to Jeff because of her strong resemblance to her mother. She also had a sweet, gentle way with Sergei he'd found endearing. But when she'd kissed him on the porch last night, something else had gone on. He'd felt a powerful tug on his emotions that wasn't about to go away.

Gabi hadn't asked for help getting through this life. On her own she'd faced every obstacle and had overcome them with her amazing positive outlook and tenacity. She'd made it clear, by leaving his house without telling him first, that she didn't want his help now. But she was going to get it anyway.

Chapter Six

After Jeff had been so wonderful to them over the weekend, Gabi suffered a guilty conscience for not responding to the voice mail he'd left yesterday. She'd checked the call time and noticed he'd phoned her soon after they'd left the park, leaving her a message about a barbecue at Nicky's.

She could have phoned him back, but hadn't wanted to get into a conversation with him while Ashley was listening, so forced herself to ignore it. By the time they'd reached the motel in L.A., he would have been home several hours and would have seen the letter she'd written to him, telling him of her plans. Ashley didn't fall asleep until eleven, too late for Gabi to phone him.

There'd been no call from him this morning, which meant he'd understood this had to be goodbye. In her heart of hearts she would have loved to talk to him one more time and thank him, but it was much better this way. Ashley had brought up his name several times already, wishing they could still be at his house. A phone conversation with him would only raise her expectations for another visit.

Determined to put him out of her mind, Gabi concentrated on the forthcoming meeting with her attorney. She chose to wear her pale blue, two-piece cotton suit with short sleeves, and bone-colored, low-slung heels, the kind of outfit she normally wore for back-to-school night.

Ashley picked out her own clothes, pink shorts and a pink flowered top with white sandals. She brought her bag of art supplies with her and some treats. Together they got out of the car and entered the foyer of Mr. Steel's office building, an older structure, not at all imposing. His suite was on the second floor.

After ushering Ashley inside, Gabi asked her to sit down while she approached a fortyish-looking, blonde receptionist she didn't recognize. She looked at the nameplate. "Good morning, Mrs. Carey. I have a ten-o'clock appointment with Mr. Steel. My name is Gabi Rafferty."

"You're right on time, Mrs. Rafferty."

"I had to bring my daughter," she said in a low voice. "Ashley doesn't know what this is about yet. She'll just sit in the chair and draw until I come out. I hope that's all right."

"No problem." The woman winked. "We keep orange sodas on hand."

"That's very nice of you."

The receptionist smiled. "Mr. Steel told me to send you right in when you arrived."

"Thank you." Gabi walked back to Ashley. "I shouldn't be long, honey."

"Okay. But hurry."

"I promise."

After giving her a kiss on top of her head, she hurried to the door at the right of the reception area and went inside. The man behind the desk got to his feet.

"It's good to see you again, Mrs. Rafferty." They shook hands. "You're looking well. Please sit down."

"Thank you."

Gabi took a seat opposite his desk. In his sixties by now, Mr. Steel had lost some hair over the past eight years, and what little he had left had gone pure silver. But he still had the aura of a man she could trust. "You seem unchanged, which is very reassuring to me."

His gray eyes crinkled as he smiled. "Your lie is most welcome. Now to get down to business." He put on his glasses. "Yesterday a courier delivered papers from your ex-husband's attorney, Mr. Durham. He's seeking joint custody of Ashley."

"He can't!" she cried, shooting to her feet. "He signed away his parental rights at the time of the divorce."

"I understand how you feel. Sit down and calm yourself so we can talk this through."

"I'm sorry." She did his bidding, but the trembling wouldn't stop. "Why didn't the final divorce decree prevent this?"

"Because those orders pertained to the divorce. Since then his circumstances have changed, and he thinks he can win by opening up a new case."

"*How* have they changed?" she cried.

"For one thing, your ex-husband has remarried and is living in an apartment in Pasadena."

"What?" she gasped. Her knuckles turned white as she clung to the arms of the armchair. When Bev had told her Ryan was looking for her, Gabi hadn't considered he might have a wife.

"I'll read what's been dictated here by Mr. Durham." The lawyer cleared his throat. "'After joining the military, my client, Mr. Ryan Rafferty, discovered he and his first wife were expecting a child. He had fears he might not survive the war and didn't want to leave his widow burdened, thus the reason he wanted her to get an abortion. When she refused, they divorced and he was deployed.'

"'During the war he received an injury that prevents him from impregnating a woman again. He has been given an honorable discharge from the service and is now married and employed at Ersher's Aviation in Pasadena as a hydraulics specialist.'

"'The couple is childless and wants to make a beautiful home for his daughter. Said couple is prepared to buy a house in Rosemead to be near said child and make up for the lost years.'"

Gabi shook her head. "He lied to his attorney about the reason he wanted me to get an abortion. I can't believe this is happening." Tears gushed down her face. "He couldn't possibly win, could he? What about the abuse?"

He removed his glasses. "I'll get to that in a minute. Naturally, I can't predict an outcome of any court case, so it will depend on all the circumstances involved. But let me say this. Since he signed away all his rights the first time, it's possible the court will consider it final and deny him any rights. It will be up to them to decide."

Gabi buried her face in her hands.

"In my opinion, for what it's worth, it's doubtful he could get joint custody, considering his past history and knowing what we do about his abuse problem, which I will bring up and have thoroughly investigated. I'll be subpoenaing anything that shows up on his military record. Rest assured no court is just going to send a seven-year-old child to a stranger because he happens to be the biological father.

"However, it's possible that, because of his inability to impregnate his wife due to his injuries, he could sway the court enough to get some form of supervised visitation. But before that happens, your daughter would have to talk to the judge, and strict guidelines would be followed.

"If your ex-husband and your daughter were to establish a relationship, it might be possible he could get regular visitation rights. At that point he would be liable for child support."

Gabi lifted her head. "I don't want his money. I don't want him anywhere near Ashley."

Mr. Steel sat back in his swivel chair. "Bear with me for a moment, Mrs. Rafferty. I'll be the one to reveal his real reasons for not wanting a baby in the first place. After both sides have given testimony, Mr. Durham will sum up the case. It will go something like this. 'I'd like to remind you that this wounded vet's life has dramatically changed since the time he was married before being deployed, that he has had an epiphany during the war and wants a relationship with his flesh-and-blood daughter. That he's now home, having been honorably discharged, and has a solid job, has remarried and has agreed to go to counseling for his past spousal-abuse problem. Search your heart and conscience before rendering a verdict.'"

Gabi's jaw hardened. "No doubt there'll be some jurors who'll want to give him a second chance."

"That's right. It will be up to me to represent your concern over his intolerance of your wanting to keep the baby, the discrepancy in his lies and, of course, his abuse. Those issues run deep. I intend to have them examined by an expert to learn why your ex-husband had such a violent reaction to the pregnancy. I'm convinced there are underlying problems that must be dealt with."

"I agree."

"Therefore, at the show-cause hearing, I'll insist that Mr. Rafferty undergo psychiatric counseling for anger management and other deep-seated issues for a period of one year before he petitions the court again to see his daughter. During that period, we're asking for a gag order to prevent him from coming anywhere near you or Ashley."

"What if he tries anyway?"

"Then the judge will throw out the case. After that, if your ex-husband tried to come near, we would have him arrested."

Gabi clasped her hands nervously. She had a lot to think about. Even with a restraining order, Mr. Steel couldn't guarantee that Ryan wouldn't try to approach Ashley. That meant Gabi had to have a serious talk with her daughter after they went out to the car.

For all she knew, Ryan could be waiting for them when they drove up to the apartment in Rosemead. Under the circumstances, Gabi had no choice but to prepare Ashley. She dreaded it, but the time had come.

"Will the judge honor your request that Ryan get psychiatric help for a year?"

"I wish I could give you an unequivocal yes."

"In other words, he can rule the way he wants," she said in a wooden voice.

"When your ex-husband's first attorney is deposed to get his testimony about the abuse, depending on the findings, the judge might feel that six months rather than a year will be sufficient time to decide if supervised visitation is indicated. Then again, he may decide to rule in your favor and the case will be closed."

"Until the next time," she muttered heatedly.

"No. Be assured there can't be a next time. The good news is you won't have to appear at the first hearing, which is scheduled for next Monday. Mr. Durham pushed hard to get this early date."

Gabi swallowed hard. "Thank heaven for that. It would be horrible to be in this kind of limbo much longer."

"I know. Is there anything else you want to ask me?"

"Can we stop him from bothering my former foster mother?"

"That's already been written in. Is there anything else you want me to add to our response before I send the papers to Mr. Durham? He'll receive them today and notify your ex-husband within the next twelve hours. That's the agreement."

"As far as I can tell, you've covered everything I've been worried about except your fee," she murmured.

"Could I work out a payment schedule with you?" If not, she would have to apply for a loan at her credit union.

"Why don't we use the same one as before?"

"That's incredibly generous of you."

"You're a courageous woman and mother. I'm on your side. Keep up that fighting spirit."

"I will. Thank you, Mr. Steel."

"After the hearing, I'll phone you immediately and let you know what transpired."

"I can't ask for more than that."

She said goodbye and walked out of his office, trying to prepare herself for the difficult conversation that lay ahead with Ashley. But she took only a few steps before she saw that her daughter wasn't alone.

The hunky male seated next to her, coloring just as madly on his own drawing pad, was unmistakable, but there was no uniform today. He'd dressed in a navy crew-neck shirt and white cargo pants.

Gabi gasped. *"Jeff?"*

"Mommy!" her daughter cried, her blue eyes radiating happiness. "He decided to surprise us. Look at my baby bear! Jeff drew a moose!"

On legs that felt like jelly, Gabi managed to reach them without toppling over. Jeff lifted his handsome head and their gazes fused. "I figured you needed someone to keep Ashley company while you conducted important business."

Joy exploded inside her, breaking through the darkness. "You've been out here all this time?"

Ashley nodded. "He came after you went in that

other room. We've done pictures of Sergei and frogs and beavers."

"Do you mind?" he asked quietly, his question obviously meant for Gabi.

Her eyelids prickled from too much emotion. "How can you even ask that question?"

His expression sobered. "Because you didn't invite me to come here."

She pressed a hand against her heart, which was thudding hard. "H-how did you get the time off?" she stammered, absolutely shocked he'd shown up like this.

"Ranger Jarvis told him he could come, Mommy. That's his boss. He's taking care of Sergei." Her daughter seemed to know a lot more about Jeff than Gabi did. "Do you like my baby bear?"

It was almost impossible to tear her eyes away from Jeff's long enough to concentrate on anything else. "He's very cute."

Jeff lifted his moose for her perusal. "What do you think about mine? I came across him at the park and named him Bullwinkle." Ashley started giggling.

One look at his picture and Gabi burst into laughter. Jeff had always been a good draftsman, like his father. He'd drawn a big black male moose with a huge rack. The animal was caught in the front seat of a car with his head sticking out the broken windshield. The steering wheel dangled from the right side of his antlers.

"Jeff said the moose ran into a parked car and couldn't get out. Isn't that funny, Mommy?"

"Hilarious."

"Did you know they can get really mean? His friend

Cal had to tranquilize it and it took four rangers to pull him into the woods. When he woke up, he ran away."

By now Mrs. Carey was laughing, too. Gabi introduced her to Jeff, explaining that he was a ranger at Yosemite Park.

The two shook hands. "That's one of my favorite places."

"Mine, too!" Ashley piped up.

"Uh-oh. There's the phone. It was nice to meet all of you."

While the receptionist dashed back to her desk, Gabi started putting all the art supplies into the bag. As Jeff helped her, their hands brushed, sending rivulets of delight through her body.

In a low aside, he said, "Why don't I follow you back to your motel?"

She shook her head. "I already checked out before we drove over here."

"Then we'll go to lunch, where we can talk. There's an In and Out Burger across the street. Unless, of course, you've already made plans with Don or Greg."

"We don't have any plans, do we, Mommy?"

He'd been talking with Ashley, who was a treasure trove of knowledge when she wanted to be. You just had to possess the right key, turn the lock and voilà.

"Not until after we've eaten. A hamburger sounds good."

By tacit agreement they left the building and made their way to the restaurant on the other side of the busy street. Ashley monopolized the conversation throughout lunch. When it was over Jeff pulled three quarters from his pocket and handed them to her.

"Over by the door I saw a machine that holds jaw-breakers."

"I know. I *love* them."

"So do I. Would you like to get us both one?"

She nodded. "Thanks, but what about Mommy?"

"She doesn't like them." His gaze flicked to Gabi's. "At least she didn't use to. Ask the cashier for a couple of chocolate mints."

"Okay." Ashley slid off the chair. "I'll be right back."

The second she ran off, Jeff looked at Gabi. "Quick, before she returns. Are you going back to Rosemead now?"

"Yes."

He grimaced. "I don't care what happened in that meeting this morning. It's still not safe for you and Ashley, otherwise you wouldn't have stayed at a motel last night."

"I can't keep hiding, Jeff. As soon as we get home, I plan to tell her everything. We have to live our lives."

"When's your first court hearing?"

"Next Monday, but I don't have to appear."

"In that amount of time your ex-husband could come around and harass you, or worse."

He wasn't about to let this go. "Ryan is being put under a restraining order. If he should show up, Mr. Steel says he'll be arrested and the case dropped for good."

Jeff shook his head. "Whatever happened in the meeting with your attorney, I know for a fact it won't be safe for you to return to Rosemead yet. I don't care what kind of restraining order is in place. We're talking about what's best for your daughter."

Her jaw clenched. "Jeff, I—"

"Come back to Yosemite and stay with me, where you have protection," he urged. "You told me yourself you don't have to start school for close to three weeks. Look at this as a long holiday. Ashley and Nicky will have the time of their lives."

"I couldn't do it to you."

"That's absurd." His voice brooked no argument. "I have a whole house going to waste. Most of the time I'm not even there. When I return my rental car to the L.A. airport, we'll put yours in long-term parking and fly back to Merced. From there we'll head back to the park in the Volvo. It's settled."

"No, Jeff…"

His jaw tightened. "That isn't what you would have said to me once."

An adrenaline rush kept her from being able to sit still. "The situation is different now."

"You're right." A bleak look had entered his eyes, bewildering her. "We're both free and over eighteen. Bev's no longer a threat to either of us."

His words stopped her cold. "What do you mean? Your *father* was the one who—"

"Shh. I'll explain later. Your daughter's coming."

Before she knew it, Jeff had gotten out of the booth and swept Ashley up in his strong arms. "Where are our jawbreakers?"

"Right here, but they didn't have any mints, Mommy."

"That's all right, honey."

Jeff looked at the two balls. "Which color do you want?"

"Blue."

"Good, because I like green. Can I have it now?"

"Yes."

"Let's stick them in our mouths together. One, two, three!" With a little laugh, she put one in his, the other in her own.

Gabi remembered him pulling that trick on her with cinnamon hots before kissing her without stopping. So many memories were streaming back unbidden.

"Do you still have the last quarter?"

"Yes." Ashley's cheek bulged.

"Let's get one for Nicky on our way out."

"But he's not here."

"I thought you could take it to him. How would you and your mother like to go back to the park with me?"

Ashley's eyes rounded. "You mean *now?*"

"I mean *right* now."

The explosion of excitement in those blue depths before her daughter hugged Jeff haunted Gabi, because the one thing she'd hoped wouldn't happen *had*. Ashley had bonded with Jeff in a very real way. Gabi didn't want to think about how painful life would be when it came time for them to leave him and the park a second time.

"Can we call Nicky and see if he can come over?"

Ashley's question couldn't have been more welcome. Jeff had just pulled in the garage after their drive from Merced. Gabi had insisted on paying for her and

Ashley's flight from L.A. He'd decided not to argue with her. She'd come back to the park with him, and at the moment, that was all that mattered.

"Sure we can, just as soon as we get your bags inside the house."

"It's dinnertime, honey," Gabi reminded her. "His parents might have other plans for him."

"If he can't come, can we go get Sergei?"

Jeff climbed out of the car. He went around to help Gabi, then opened the back door for Ashley. "I'll call Chase and find out." After pulling the bags from the trunk, he opened the door into the house and the three of them walked through to the kitchen.

He liked the feeling of togetherness so much he could taste it. The knowledge that Gabi and her daughter would be his guests for the next few weeks—unless, heaven forbid, something unforeseen happened—gave him a brand-new reason to be alive. The woman he'd thought lost to him forever had turned up again. He wasn't about to lose her a second time.

They needed to talk, but couldn't do it around Ashley. Once she had friends to play with, and was out of earshot, he could explain certain truths to Gabi. The reference to Bev had slipped out at the restaurant. Probably a Freudian slip, since he wanted Gabi to be apprised of all the facts, now that she'd met with her attorney.

Without hesitation he phoned Chase.

"Jeff? What are you doing calling me? I didn't expect to hear from you this soon."

"Plans have changed. I wanted you to know I'm back."

"That was a fast trip."

Alone for a minute, because the Raffertys had disappeared into another part of the house, he said, "Thanks for making it possible. I've brought Gabi and Ashley back with me. They'll be staying at the house for a few weeks."

"Nice. Another friend for the kids to play with." Chase never pried and was always discreet.

"Exactly. Do you think Roberta will be upset if I drive over to pick up Sergei now?"

"Tell you what. We just finished eating and she's out in front doing tricks with him. It might be better if I tell her you're back, and let her decide to walk Sergei over to your house on her own. I'll bring his stuff by in a little while."

"Great. Thanks, Chase."

After they hung up, he decided to phone the Rossiters. Rachel picked up on the second ring. "Hi, Jeff! What a surprise! We heard you'd be gone from the park for a few days."

"My plans changed and I'm back with Gabi and Ashley. They'll be here for a few weeks."

"Bless you," she whispered. "That news couldn't make me happier. Ever since Gabi dropped Nicky off at the house, he's been grumpy and difficult. Kind of like he was before Vance and I got together. I thought those days were over. My husband and I have been racking our brains trying to figure out what's gotten into him."

Jeff knew exactly what was wrong with Nicky. It was the effect Gabi and her daughter had on the male of the species, young or old.

"Is he there?"

"No. Vance took him to Wawona for a special father-and-son evening. I don't expect them home before dark. I can't wait till they get back so I can tell him. Ask Gabi to bring her daughter over in the morning with Sergei."

"I will. Thanks, Rachel."

"Hey—I'm the one who needs to thank you. This means peace around the house until your guests leave again. But I don't want to think about that right now."

Neither did Jeff. He hung up, realizing he was going to have to take this a day at a time.

When he walked through the house, he found his two favorite people in the spare bedroom containing Sergei's crate and the cot. Ashley was helping her mother put clean sheets on the latter. He shot Gabi a questioning glance.

"Ashley wants to stay in here with Sergei. Is that all right with you? I'll sleep in the living room on the pullout couch."

"Whatever makes you happy. The couch is already made up." Though he preferred she use his bed, he kept his mouth shut. As long as she was willing to sleep anywhere beneath his roof, he wasn't going to question her choices. It was a miracle she was here at all.

"Do you want both suitcases in here?"

"Please. I'll use this room to change."

"I'll get them."

He went back to the kitchen to gather everything, including the bag holding Ashley's art supplies. As he deposited them in the spare bedroom, they all heard the doorbell ring.

"I think that's Roberta. Come and meet her," Jeff suggested."

The next few minutes passed in a blur as Chase's brunette daughter came in the house with Sergei. The dog made a dive for Ashley, causing everyone to laugh. Soon their little group got acquainted.

Though five years older, Roberta didn't seem to mind the age difference. Ashley acted perfectly comfortable with her, even showing her the drawings they'd made at the lawyer's office. They were engrossed in conversation when Chase came by to deliver Sergei's stuff and take his daughter home. He related more animal stories that had everyone laughing.

Several times Gabi flashed Jeff a look that told him she liked the intelligent girl and her father. That was a plus for a lot of reasons, not the least of which was Jeff's hope that Gabi would find it difficult, if not impossible, to consider leaving the park when the time came.

After the Jarvises left, Gabi took Ashley to the bedroom to help her get ready for bed. A few minutes later the dark-haired pixie came out to the living room wearing Princess Aurora pajamas. Sergei trailed her.

Before Jeff understood her intentions, she ran over to him and gave him a hug. "I wish I could live here forever."

"So do I, sweetheart." His response came straight from his heart as he rocked her. Over her slender shoulder his eyes caught the haunted look in Gabi's as she hesitated in the center of the room.

"Ashley?"

She turned to her mother while still pressed against Jeff. "What is it?"

"We're just visiting for a little while."

"I know."

"Come to bed now, honey. I need to talk to you about something very important before you go to sleep."

"Can Jeff come, too?"

He saw the struggle Gabi was having, trying to broach the subject of Ashley's father, but knew she wanted to be alone.

"Guess what? I need to take Sergei out for a walk before he goes to bed. But I'll be back soon."

"Okay."

Jeff reached for the leash Roberta had left on the coffee table. "Come on, Sergei. Let's go."

GABI APPRECIATED Jeff's sensitivity. She walked over to the couch and slipped off her heels before curling up on the end of it with her legs tucked beneath her. "Come here, honey."

Ashley sat down next to her. "What is it?"

"We've never talked much about your father because he went away so long ago. I didn't know if he would ever come back, but the other day I found out he's no longer in the military. He got married and is living in Pasadena, not that far away from our apartment in Rosemead."

Her daughter got to her feet, but didn't say anything.

"The reason I had to go see Mr. Steel in Los Angeles today is because I found out your father wants to see you."

"He does?" Ashley stared at her for the longest time, obviously shaken by the news. How much a seven-year-old could absorb about her absentee father was anyone's guess.

"Yes." By now Gabi was praying for inspiration. "The thing is, he's been gone such a long time, he needs to get permission to see you."

"How come?"

"Because we have rules in our country. He hasn't been here all these years to help me take care of you while you've been growing up. Now that he wants to see you, he has to go through a judge who will decide if he can see you or not.

"The judge will want to talk to you and find out how you feel. Your father is supposed to wait until the judge tells him what he can or can't do, but he might decide to try to see you anyway."

Her blue eyes teared up. "Is my father nice like Jeff?"

Help.

"Do you know what? It's been so many years since I last saw him, I have no idea what's he's like now. When I married him, I loved him very much, but our marriage didn't last and we got a divorce."

"Why did you get a divorce?"

"Because we wanted different things. He liked being a soldier. I wanted to be a mommy."

"Oh."

The famous *oh.*

"Before the judge decides anything, I wanted you to know the truth so you're prepared in case your father comes to the apartment or to your school after we get back to Rosemead."

"I don't want to go back."

"Honey—that's where we live. I teach school there. Your friends are there, like Jessica. But we'll enjoy our vacation here first."

"I want to stay with Jeff."

In the next breath she ran out of the living room. Gabi realized her daughter was reacting to news she hadn't had time to process yet. Jeff was the only man she'd ever been around for any length of time. A few hours at a movie or dinner with Greg or Don didn't count.

Naturally, she would turn to Jeff. She couldn't comprehend having another man in her life. Before Gabi had brought up the subject tonight, Ashley had already told Jeff she wanted to live here forever. Her father was a total stranger to her.

Only now did it occur to Gabi that Ashley had always been silent on the subject of her father. As far as she could tell, her daughter hadn't been that curious about him. Maybe that was Gabi's fault, because she hadn't encouraged her to talk about him.

But not all children were the same. A certain percentage of Gabi's students came from divorced families, and she'd noticed that some of them had more anxiety over or more natural interest in the parent they didn't live with than others.

As she jumped up from the couch to follow Ashley, Jeff came through the front door with Sergei. He studied her expression. "I take it the talk with Ashley didn't go well."

"To be truthful, I have no idea how it went. I think she's in shock, but I couldn't put it off any longer."

"You did the right thing. Forewarned is forearmed.

Maybe Sergei can provide the comfort she needs to-night. Let's go in to her and say good-night."

Gabi nodded. Together they joined her daughter, who'd climbed under the covers of the cot, clutching Mr. Charles. Gabi hadn't seen her to do that for quite a while. It meant she'd searched through her suitcase to find him.

Gabi walked to one side of the bed, Jeff to the other. He smiled down at the child. "I've brought you a friend."

"Will Sergei climb up here with me?"

"Why don't you find out? Pat the mattress and ask him."

"Okay. Come here, Sergei. Come on."

The dog immediately responded and found a spot at her feet.

"He came!"

"Of course. He'll protect you all night."

A sweet smile broke out on her face. She looked at Gabi. "Good night, Mommy. I love you."

She leaned over to kiss her. "I love you, too, honey. I'll leave the door open. If you need me during the night, just come into the living room."

"Aren't you going to bed?"

"In a few minutes. I want to talk to Jeff first."

"Okay." Ashley's gaze switched to his. "Good night, Jeff. Thanks for letting Sergei sleep with me."

"He wouldn't want to be anywhere else. Good night."

Chapter Seven

Gabi followed Jeff out of the room and down the hall. On the way to the living room he pulled a pillow from the linen closet. "Are you hungry? Thirsty?" he asked.

"Neither, thank you."

He opened the couch bed for her and put the pillow on top.

She sank down on one of the chairs. "All you do is wait on me and Ashley. My debt to you is building. How did you know where to find us in L.A.?"

"By process of elimination. I knew your attorney's name."

Gabi sat forward, clasping her hands together. "Why did you get time off and follow us there? The truth now."

He sat on the couch arm and looked down at her. In the semidarkness his rugged features stood out. "I'm glad you said that, because we not only have unfinished business between us, it's time you knew the whole truth about the past."

She pressed her lips together. "You said something

about Bev no longer being a threat. How did she pose one?"

Jeff's expression darkened. "It's true Dad wanted to stop things before they went too far with you and me. But it was Bev who, along with Nora's and Ellen's help, did the real damage that made it impossible for me to go on living at home."

Gabi smoothed the curls away from her cheeks. "What are you saying?"

"It's going to hurt you, because you liked Bev better than the other foster parents you'd lived with."

Gabi started to get a sick feeling inside. "What did she do?"

"After I left Alhambra, there's only one reason I didn't try to get in touch with you, Gabi. One afternoon before you got home from school, I was in the garage working on my motorcycle when Bev suddenly appeared. It was the day before my high-school graduation. Nora's, too."

"I remember. At lunch we wrote letters to each other in our yearbooks."

He nodded. "Ellen must have let Bev in the house and told her where to find me. No one else was around. My dad hadn't come home from work yet. I thought it was weird. Let's face it—she never liked me."

"That's because Nora was her favorite."

"Nora was jealous of you, Gabi. But I didn't know how jealous until Bev told me Nora had seen you and me in bed together numerous times. Because you were a minor, Bev said she had enough evidence to send you back through the court system unless I moved out of my dad's house."

Pain drove Gabi to her feet. "No!"

"It's true. I knew how you'd suffered over the years, being shuffled from one foster home to another. There was no way I was going to let her do that to you, so I left."

She shook her head. "I don't believe it."

"It got uglier," he muttered. "Bev never was quite the same after Ron died."

"Her husband's death was very hard on her, but to threaten you..."

"She could see how close you and I were getting. I'd just turned eighteen. Nora's eighteenth birthday would be coming up soon and she'd be long gone. I knew how Bev's mind worked. She was afraid I'd talk you into running away with me. That meant she'd lose the best babysitter she ever had for Monte. It also meant she'd lose money."

"I know. She counted on every penny."

"Without the government payment she received once a month for the three of you, she couldn't have made it. With Nora on the verge of leaving, she'd have to wait to get another foster child. In the meantime she depended on the money from you and Monte. In her fear, she convinced my dad and Ellen that *I* had to leave home, to put a permanent halt to things."

"It's so hard to believe."

Jeff moved off the end of the couch and stood in front of her. "All you have to do is pick up the phone and ask Bev."

Gabi looked away from him. "I—I know you're telling me the truth. It's just that I don't want to be-lieve it."

"Neither did I at the time. Her final words to me were the coup de grace. If I as much as made one phone call, or tried to see you on the sly, or write you a postcard or send an email, then she'd carry out her threat and involve the police.

"My dad backed her because he didn't want me being accused of rape and dragged into court over your case. You don't mess with a juvenile. He told me I'd better move out fast before Bev made good on her threat."

"But Nora lied!"

"That was her way of getting back at me for never being interested in her. In a court of law it would have been her word against yours. They all had their motives, Gabi. Your foster mother didn't want to lose the money she would continue to receive as long as you stayed under her roof until you turned eighteen.

"Ellen was a selfish woman and jealous of the way Dad had felt about my mother. My stepmother didn't like me and wanted me out of the house so she could have him to herself. She became a willing accomplice for Bev. Dad just wanted peace and believed my leaving home was the only solution."

Hot tears rolled down Gabi's cheeks. "I didn't know Bev could be that cruel." Bev...who'd supported her decision to divorce Ryan. Who'd phoned her the other day to tell her Ryan was back and looking for her. Did one person ever really know another?

"Not cruel, Gabi." He put his arms around her and pulled her close against his hard body. "Desperate," he whispered into her hair. "How else could she hold on to the life she'd made for herself?"

"But it meant *you* had to leave home. I know how

much you loved your father. I can't bear it that you were forced to go away because of Bev." Gabi couldn't hold back any longer and sobbed quietly against his shoulder.

He smoothed his hands over her back to comfort her.

"Oh, Jeff... I can't fathom that she would let me suffer like I did and never once let on *she* was the reason you left. No wonder she didn't tell me you came back to see me when I turned eighteen. After what she'd done to us, she didn't dare." Gabi's voice shook.

He clasped her tighter, kissing the top of her head. As she melted against him, she became aware she was enjoying being in his arms way too much. Fearing he knew it, Gabi eased away from him, not wanting him to think she was taking advantage of the situation. They weren't the same two people anymore.

"It's a fact she'd be in shock if she knew we were together now."

Gabi wiped the tears away with the palms of her hands. "Finally, I have the truth. If it weren't for your picture in the paper..."

He rubbed the back of his neck, a gesture she'd seen him make before when he was pondering something important. "I believe we have Sergei to thank for his part in our reunion."

"Yes," Gabi murmured. "Ashley cried, 'Look at his pointy ears!' and suddenly there you were, providing the safety I'd instinctively sought. No one ever had a better friend."

She heard Jeff's deep intake of breath. "At least Bev couldn't take that away from us."

"No. Maybe sometime soon, before Ashley and I go home to Rosemead, you'll tell me what you did in the intervening years before you ended up in Yosemite. I'd like to hear everything, but not tonight. After this long, draining day, we both need sleep. Good night."

Gabi hurried to Ashley's room to get ready for bed. Another few seconds and she would have melted into his arms, the way she'd once done. For old times' sake it would have been easy enough to do, because he'd provided her a refuge.

But they'd lived apart from each other for many years. He'd been married and divorced, too. The painful adage that you could never go home again was in play here.

ONCE JEFF HAD LOCKED UP, he went to bed, cognizant of the wind blowing around the corners of the house. The eerie whistling beneath the eaves gave proof of a microburst growing in momentum. He had the impression the elements were doing their worst to tear off his roof.

Earlier in the day, after he'd landed at the Merced airport with Gabi and Ashley and they'd eaten another meal, he'd noticed the shape of the clouds and had sensed a thunderstorm building over the high Sierras, headed for the park.

The summer storms could be particularly violent over El Capitan and Half Dome. When nature did her worst, those were the times a terrible emptiness stole through him and he felt his aloneness as a tangible thing...perhaps the way Adam might have felt without Eve.

But since Gabi had come to the park last Saturday, everything had changed. Tonight she lay just a few feet away, in the living room, her daughter in the spare bedroom. Their presence brought him a contentment he'd never known before. Though the rains were now descending in a deluge, he experienced a warm sensation the likes of which he'd never felt in his life. Tomorrow he had plans for them....

But no sooner had he closed his eyes than the blare of the phone jerked him out of his euphoric state. He groaned as he reached for the receiver, noting it was five after one in the morning. "Thompson here."

"Jeff, it's Chase. The National Weather Service says heavy rains in the Sierra Nevada are causing flash floods in rivers and streams throughout the whole area. Golf-ball-size hail has been reported. Rangers are calling in with reports of four inches of water on the ground already in some campgrounds. I've just given the order to close the road into Yosemite Valley."

Jeff let out a whistle. "Where do you want me?"

"I need you to help evacuate the campers from Camp Four to the Yosemite Lodge stat! Finlay will be joining you."

"I'm on my way!"

In his closet he kept his protective clothing the rangers called hurry-ups. He put everything on including his waders and hooded parka. The rest of the equipment he would need was in his truck. As soon as he was ready, he hurried through to the living room and woke Gabi.

"Jeff?" She sat up, looking sleepy and appealing in a T-shirt he hadn't seen before.

"Shh." He put a finger to her lips. "I don't want to

wake up Ashley. The storm we saw earlier has hit and there's been flooding. I have to go help some campers to dry ground, but you're safe here. Call me if you get worried about anything. I'll be back as soon as I can."

Without her permission he kissed her swiftly on the mouth, before dashing through the house to the garage. The taste of her stayed with him all the way to the village.

Arriving at his destination, he jumped down into six inches of water and opened the tailgate of the truck for the first load of campers to get in. You could be forgiven for not knowing where you were in these monsoonlike conditions.

He dug into his work. After seeing the last of the campers into the lodge, Jeff reported in and was told to help evacuate more at the Lower Pines Campground. They were to be taken to the Ahwahnee Hotel.

By four in the morning the rain had turned into a light drizzle, its damage done. The good news from Chase was that all campers in the valley had been sheltered and were accounted for. Better yet, there'd been no serious injuries reported. Everyone was to assemble at headquarters to plan cleanup operations.

The flooding meant Jeff's team would need to inspect the damage to all roads, buildings and bridges. Once he could verify the integrity of the structures and order repairs for those that had been compromised, he could get back to new projects he'd been working on.

He sloshed back to his truck in at least eight inches of water and drove over to headquarters, pulling up alongside Vance, who was just getting out of his truck.

The chief looked as tired as Jeff felt, but he hadn't lost his sense of humor. "At least our home away from home is still here."

"Amen." They both chuckled as they realized the water hadn't quite reached the top of the building's foundation. "Before you became a ranger, you lived next door to the park all your life. Did you ever see it do this before?"

Vance shook his head. "No, but years ago, I understand, a storm flooded the valley floor three feet. I guess we got off lucky tonight." They entered through the back door. "Did I tell you I'm glad you're back with you-know-who? Otherwise I might have had a *real* emergency on my hands with Nicky."

Thoughts of getting home to Gabi and Ashley had kept Jeff's adrenaline surging throughout the night. He grinned in spite of the mess facing them. "Rachel told me."

Vance's eyebrows lifted. "Did she also tell you he wants me to give Gabi a job like I gave Cal's wife? Then Ashley will *have* to live at the park," the chief said, imitating his son.

Jeff laughed so hard that the two bedraggled-looking rangers who'd just come in behind them wanted to know how anything could be funny after such a wretched night.

Vance winked at Jeff. "Just a little private joke between Ranger Thompson and me."

Nicky Darrow Rossiter. Probably the funniest and most creative young inhabitant at Yosemite. Jeff liked the way he thought. But where Gabi was concerned, Jeff was leap years ahead of him.

GABI WAS THE FIRST ONE UP. She checked her watch. Ten to eight. Had Jeff come back while she'd been sleeping? Before she dared peek in on him in his bedroom, she rolled out of bed and hurried through the house to the garage, but his truck was missing. Maybe it was out in the driveway.

She raced through to the living room. When she opened the front door, she discovered the street and Jeff's yard were under several inches of water and there was no sign of his truck. The water had risen to the bottom step of the porch.

Incredible!

Gabi looked up at the sky. The storm had passed over, leaving a trail of pink-tinted clouds as the sun rose. It promised to be a beautiful day, but the damage from flooding like this would be horrendous. Every ranger would be busy taking care of stranded tourists, not to mention other emergencies involving campers and vehicles. She shivered just thinking about it.

While she stood there taking in the unexpected sight, Ashley and Sergei joined her. Gabi slid an arm around her daughter and pulled her close. "Can you believe what that thunderstorm brought?"

"I didn't hear it rain."

"That's because you were too tired."

"Where's Jeff?"

She touched her fingers to her lips where Jeff had kissed her last night before he'd left. Or had she just imagined it? "He's out helping people who got caught in the downpour."

"Oh. Can we call Nicky? I want to go out in the water and play."

"Before we do anything like that, we need to get dressed and have breakfast. By then Jeff will have phoned me and we'll make plans." Hopefully, he was all right. Of course he would be. This was the kind of work he loved. Still...

"Okay. Come on, Sergei."

Gabi had just shut the door when her cell phone rang, causing her pulse to race. She reached for it on the coffee table where she'd left her purse, and clicked on. "Jeff?"

"No." There was a prolonged silence before the female voice said, "It's Bev."

Gabi's lungs froze.

How could she have been so foolish to answer the phone like that without checking the caller ID first? The fact that Bev didn't ask if the Jeff she assumed was calling was the same Jeff who'd once lived next door to them revealed her culpability. Gabi drew in a deep breath.

"Has Ryan been harassing you again?"

"He called me a few minutes ago demanding to know where you are. I thought you'd spoken to your attorney."

"I did. In fact, I met with him yesterday. We've sent his attorney our response. By now Ryan should have had a phone call telling him to stay away from you. In bothering you, he's now breaking the law. As soon as we hang up I'll phone Mr. Steel and tell him what's happened. If his attorney can't stop him, then Ryan will be arrested."

"Maybe *you* need to phone Ryan."

The gloves were off. Gabi shouldn't be surprised, not

after what Jeff had revealed. At this stage, her former foster mom was an enigma to her.

Though Gabi had no intention of contacting Ryan, she decided to placate her. "Just a minute, Bev. I need to get my purse." She searched for pen and paper. "Okay. Go ahead and give me his number."

While she was writing it down, she heard the garage door open. Her heart quaked because it meant Jeff was home. Ashley raced through the house with Sergei to greet him.

"I'm sorry you've been bothered, Bev. I'll take steps to make sure you don't hear from him again. Now I have to go."

Gabi hung up and hurried out of the living room. Once she'd reached the guest bathroom, she took off the long T-shirt she'd slept in, and showered. Afterward she dressed in jeans and a layered aqua cotton top.

Before she joined the others, she phoned her attorney. He wasn't in, so she left a message with the receptionist for him to call her.

"Don't come too close," Jeff said as she entered the kitchen a few minutes later. Sergei had gone to his corner to eat.

"You have to be beyond exhaustion!"

He sighed. "That's a fact. I'm afraid I frightened Ashley. She's outside with Nicky, sloshing around in her flip-flops. Samson stayed home this time." Jeff was eating a tuna sandwich.

"You haven't outgrown your love of tuna. Why am I not surprised?" she murmured.

His grin turned her heart over. Overnight he'd grown a beard, and his hazel eyes were heavy-lidded. But Gabi thought he'd never looked more appealing, standing there with disheveled hair, a white T-shirt covering his well-defined chest.

"If you'd phoned, I would've had breakfast waiting for you."

He shook his head before swallowing the rest of his orange juice, drawing her attention to his biceps with their farmer tan. Though not a bodybuilder, he'd been well developed even in high school. It took powerful arms to handle his motorcycle over ground where only a daredevil would go. "This is what I crave when I've been out all night."

She checked her watch. "You haven't had any sleep for twenty-six hours. Go to bed and I'll take care of everything else."

His eyes narrowed. "Promise to be here when I wake up?"

She deserved that. "Where would I go with a virtual lake surrounding us?"

A sensual smile broke out on his attractive face. "You wouldn't get far. Chase closed the road leading in and out of Yosemite Valley, but have no fear. The water is already starting to recede. By the time I wake up, the kids will be able to find all kinds of stuff in the grass. Nicky can't wait."

Gabi studied Jeff's handsome features. Who knew what kind of emergencies he'd had to deal with during the night? "What can I do for you? If you'll leave your clothes outside the bedroom door, I'll wash them for you."

"I won't say no to an offer like that. Every part of me is filthy, including my T-shirt. Which reminds me.

Come to my room with me. I want to give you something I've been holding on to for a long time."

Curious, she followed him out of the kitchen and down the hall. He walked over to his dresser, opened the bottom drawer and reached in between folded jeans for a sack, which he handed her.

"Happy belated high-school graduation."

It had to be the gift he'd brought her when he'd dropped by Bev's. With trembling hands Gabi opened it and pulled out a navy blue T-shirt. Holding it up, she read the message printed in white letters: Today My Life Begins.

A moan escaped her lips. She clutched the shirt to her chest, unable to breathe for a moment. By the time she dared look at him, he'd disappeared into his bathroom. She could hear the shower running.

Jeff...

Sergei wandered in and brushed against her legs. She rubbed his fur. "I know you've missed him, but we have to let him sleep. Come on. Let's go check on the children."

But first she made a detour to the guest bedroom. After folding the T-shirt and slipping it back in the sack, she put it in the bottom of her suitcase. Tears dripped inside before she could close the lid. Like the famous Pennsylvania Dutch expression, she was too soon oldt, too late schmart.

Gabi couldn't go back and rewrite history. She wished Jeff hadn't given it to her. The act had dredged up pain she didn't want to revisit.

At noon she gathered the children around the dining-room table to eat tomato soup and grilled cheese sandwiches. Then she did dishes and several loads of laundry. Twice she mopped the floor from the garage to the kitchen, after the kids traipsed in with wet feet. All in all, it was a wonderful day and there was more to come.

Rachel had phoned and invited them for the barbecue that hadn't come off the other evening. She'd planned it for six-thirty, hoping her husband would be awake by then. The chief had been working nonstop for over twenty-four hours, too.

Gabi offered to contribute deviled eggs. While she got busy making them, the kids settled down to doing artwork in the living room. Gabi couldn't remember ever being this happy before. Though this dream she was living here at the park would come to an end soon, she refused to think about that right now.

As she was about to cover the eggs with foil, Jeff's tall, hard-muscled body suddenly appeared in the kitchen, showered and clean shaven. "No, no, not yet—" He sneaked one egg from the plate and popped it in his mouth.

He'd put on a coffee-colored sport shirt and tan chinos. It gave her inestimable pleasure just to look at him while she waited to hear the verdict.

The green flecks in his eyes ignited. "That tasted exactly like my mom's."

"Ruth taught me how to make them. You mash the cooked egg yolk through a strainer before mixing it with Best Foods mayonnaise and celery seed."

"I could eat the whole plate!"

"You and the Mad Hatter."

"That's right. He'd drink tea and eat the saucers."

She smiled. "I remember. If you'd had more eggs on hand, I would have made a whole platter just for you. As it is, we're due at the Rossiters' for dinner right now. Nicky said they have a big watermelon that's ripe to eat. No doubt Rachel has made enough potato salad to satisfy you."

"Do you have Mom's recipe for potato salad memorized, too?"

"What do you think?"

His expression grew solemn. "I think I have to keep you around for the duration."

When he looked at her like that, weakness attacked her body. "If you'll get the children, I'll grab my purse and meet you at the car."

JEFF GUESSED it was too much to hope that Gabi might have put on the T-shirt he'd given her. When she'd looked at it, he knew by the sudden quiet that she'd been emotionally affected, but he couldn't read her mind.

There'd been moments since they'd come back to the park when he'd managed to forget she had an ex-husband. Denial had a lot to answer for, yet the fruit of her marriage to another man was sitting in the back seat of the Volvo with Nicky and Sergei.

Years ago she'd fallen in love with Ryan Rafferty. She'd married him, made love with him, created a home with him. He'd given her a baby.

Again Jeff had to conclude that no matter how profoundly he and Gabi had loved each other in their teens, she'd grown up and moved on. Until the judge ruled in her case about Ashley's birth father and his rights, Jeff had no hope of gaining her exclusive attention. He could be the friend she'd sought after seeing his picture in the newspaper, but would be a fool to expect anything more from her.

She's fighting for her daughter's life, Thompson.

The only thing Jeff could do was help her to achieve that end. For the time being, that meant providing her a safe haven. Nothing more.

When they reached Nicky's house, Jeff hardly recognized Vance or Chase. The last time he'd seen them had been ten hours ago, when they'd all been covered in muck.

Surprising what a difference a day made. Already the flood had pretty much receded. Jeff pulled into Vance's driveway, confident they wouldn't track water into his house.

The chief stood in the doorway. "Hey, sport!" he called.

"Hi, Dad!" Nicky answered.

"Welcome to the ark," he quipped. At that comment both Jeff and Gabi started chuckling.

Perplexed, Nicky looked up at his father. "What ark?"

"Don't you remember this morning? But a little while ago I sent out a dove, and it never came back."

"No, you didn't, Dad…."

"No?" With a laugh, he hugged Nicky and followed him through the house.

Ashley and Gabi trailed after them with Sergei. Jeff brought up the rear, carrying the eggs to the dining room, where Rachel had set up a buffet. She told them to load their plates and they'd sit around the living room to eat.

Jeff introduced Gabi to Chase's wife. "I hear you're the park's top archaeologist," Gabi said.

Annie smiled. "Let's just hope Nicky doesn't say that around my boss. It's so nice to meet you, Gabi. Roberta tells me you teach third grade in Rosemead."

"Hey—she could be *my* teacher!" Nicky cried.

"You already have an excellent one," his father reminded him.

"But Ashley's mommy would be better."

Gabi smiled. "That's very nice of you to say, but I have a group of students waiting for me to teach them. School's going to start in a couple of weeks."

"I wish we didn't have to go back," Ashley complained. "I don't want to leave Jeff's house."

"Yeah. I think you should stay on a *long* vacation," Nicky declared, entertaining Jeff no end. The boy's ears were never far away.

Gabi stood next to Annie. "Roberta told me you're expecting. Congratulations."

"We're excited, but it's a long way off yet."

"Ashley's mommy got a nosebleed yesterday, but she's not going to have a baby."

"Nicky!" both his parents said at the same time.

"That isn't something we discuss in front of company," Rachel admonished him from her spot on the couch next to Vance, who held their son, Parker. The baby was adorable and as dark-haired as Rachel was fair. Beneath those golden curls, she'd gone pink at Nicky's comment.

Jeff caught the glint of amusement in Gabi's eyes before she said, "I...bumped into the kitchen door."

"Jeff bumped into it, too," Nicky informed anyone listening.

At that point the adults broke into gales of laughter before settling down to a feast of ribs and corn on the cob. Later, after the children ate their watermelon and ran off to watch a movie in the den, the talk centered around the flooding. For once Sergei stayed by Jeff. He had an idea the dog was missing Cal. Out of compassion he gave him a doggy treat.

Vance handed Parker to his wife, then leaned forward to address Gabi, who sat in a chair opposite the couch. "Jeff tells us you two used to live next door to each other. What was he like when you were both in high school?"

Without looking at Jeff she launched in. "Well, for one thing, his father taught him a lot about the construction business. They remodeled their whole house and built a beautiful patio in the back. Jeff could fix anything."

"That's one of the reasons the park needs him," Vance commented.

"For another thing," Gabi continued, "he was the hottest Kawasaki cyclist around, and all the girls were crazy about him. My friend Kim begged me to put in a good word for her, but she had to wait in line for all the other girls dying to go for a ride with him."

Chase nodded. "So far things haven't changed."

"That's what Nicky tells me," Gabi quipped.

"Uh-oh," the chief murmured. "What did he say?"

A mysterious look crossed her face. "I'm afraid that's classified."

Everyone chuckled. Jeff got to his feet and took

empty plates to the kitchen. Sergei followed him. As he was coming back, he heard Nicky's voice.

"Mom?" He flew into the living room. "Can we have a sleepover? Roberta and Ashley want to stay here! We can put sleeping bags in my room."

"I think that sounds like fun, if Annie and Gabi say it's all right."

Jeff held his breath, waiting for Gabi's answer.

Ashley ran to her mother. "Please, Mommy?"

Gabi looked uncomfortable. "We don't have a sleeping bag for you."

"That's no problem," Annie interjected. "She can use mine. Chase will bring it over with Roberta's."

"Well, I guess, if that's what you'd like to do." Her permission was rewarded with a huge hug from Ashley.

"Hooray!" Nicky cried. "Come on. Let's go finish our movie." The three children ran out of the living room again.

"Hooray" expressed it, all right. That meant Jeff would have a whole night alone at his house with Gabi.

He got up to clear everything from the dining-room table and start the dishes. The need to keep his body moving was paramount while he waited for his heart to slow to a normal rhythm. Pretty soon the men joined him in the kitchen. They talked shop and made short work of the cleanup.

As Chase gathered the dish towels to go in the washer, he darted Jeff a glance. "Remember that favor you said you owed me? Well, I'm afraid you'll have to be on duty at headquarters tonight, because I'm short a man on the roster."

"Our skeleton crew is stretched too far," the chief added.

Both of them spoke in a deadpan voice, throwing Jeff off guard for about ten seconds before they burst into laughter that reverberated off the walls.

Chase's smile was a mile wide. "If you could see the look on your face."

It was probably the first time in his life Jeff had ever blushed.

"What's going on?" Rachel had come into the kitchen with the women.

Vance put his arm around his wife and baby. "A private joke, darling. But if—"

"No, no. I'm sure we girls are better off not hearing it. All I can say is, if it meant my dishes got done and everything is immaculate, I'm not going to complain."

"It's getting late. I'll go get the sleeping bags. Be right back." Chase kissed his wife's cheek before disappearing from the kitchen.

Jeff turned to Gabi, who'd gone quiet. "Why don't you say good-night to Ashley? I'll be out in the car."

Chapter Eight

Gabi felt Jeff's eyes on her after they walked into his kitchen from the garage. He put away the plate they'd taken over to the Rossiters'. "You were quiet all the way home. Are you worried Ashley's going to call you to come and get her?"

"No." Gabi leaned over to pat Sergei's head. "To be honest, I'm afraid she won't."

He got down the instant coffee. "Want some?"

"No, thank you."

After he'd heated his mug in the microwave, he turned to her. "Is this the first time she's ever slept away from you before?"

"Yes."

"If you want to stay over at the Rossiters', I'll take you back. I know you'll be welcome."

"I have no doubt of it. They're terrific people, but Ashley has taken a big step tonight. It's good for her."

"Unfortunately, Mom's the one suffering separation anxiety," he said with compassion. "It's perfectly understandable when she's been your whole world all these years. Let's go into the living room."

Gabi moved to the other room and sank down in one

of the chairs next to the couch. Jeff remained standing while he sipped his coffee, his free hand on his hip. After all the years apart, it was hard to believe they were alone together like this.

"You've found heaven here in Yosemite, haven't you?" Gabi said.

"Almost."

With that answer, she lowered her head. She wanted to ask him so many questions, but didn't know where to start. "How did you end up here?"

"That's a long story."

She brushed some imaginary lint off her arm. "You've been listening to me for days. Now I'm anxious to hear about your life."

"To answer your question with a short version, I worked in Hollywood as a motorcycle stunt rider. It paid me the kind of money I needed to make while I went to college for my construction engineering degree."

"So you *did* get it."

He nodded. "But I never started up my own construction company because I had too much else going on."

"I knew you were a fabulous cyclist. No wonder you were hired." After a pause, she asked, "When did you marry?"

"During my second year at college, but by the end of it, we divorced."

A pang of jealousy spread through Gabi.

"I did professional stunt riding for about five years. The last film I worked on, they were shooting the scene with me near North Fork, just sixty-odd miles south of Yosemite. The crew was there close to a week. At the end of each day's shooting, I'd ride into the park and look around. I fell in love with the place."

"I can see why," she murmured. "Ashley absolutely adores it here, too. Who wouldn't?"

He put his empty mug on the coffee table and sat down on the couch near her, stretching his long legs. It was like déjà vu seeing him relax like that. Sergei settled at his feet.

"I chatted with some of the rangers, and before I knew it, I gave up my job and went to Georgia for a session at the Federal Law Enforcement Training Center."

She took a deep breath. "You must have wanted it badly."

"You have no idea. I got hired as a ranger and worked two years at two different parks, but kept trying to get on at Yosemite. One day there was an opening and I grabbed for it."

"How long have you been here?"

"Six years."

She started counting. He'd been divorced a long time. Longer than her, actually.

"In many ways our lives have paralleled each other," Jeff said, sending her a meaningful glance. "I was married less than a year, too." He might as well be reading her mind.

Restless, Gabi shifted in the chair. "How did you meet her?"

Jeff sat forward, clasping his hands between his legs. "Fran's father owns a company that builds sets for all types of stunt-riding exhibitions. When she wasn't at film school, Fran helped at his office in L.A. We started going out and ended up married. She was a lovely person, but I'm afraid we were too different and the marriage simply didn't take."

Gabi heard genuine affection in his tone as he talked about his ex-wife. "I'm sorry it didn't work out. Did she ride, too?"

"No. Occasionally I could get her to take a run on my bike with me, but her real interest was in film. These days she works for Pacific Pictures." He smiled. "Now tell me what kind of job you took after you left Bev's."

Obviously, he wanted to change the subject. Maybe his divorce hurt him too much to talk about.

"Thanks to your mom, I developed a love for cooking and got hired by a catering firm in Los Angeles."

Jeff studied her features through veiled eyes. "How did you meet your husband?"

"At a wedding we were catering. Ryan was one of the guests."

"Was it love at first sight?"

He'd asked the question she'd wanted to ask him about Fran. It angered Gabi, but that wasn't his fault. Jeff couldn't have any comprehension of the permanent ache in her heart.

"I think that only happens to the young, don't you? Ryan was attractive and he grew on me. I never saw the change in him coming."

Talking about him caused her to shudder, and she stood up. Jeff rose to his feet and grasped her upper arms before she could turn away. "I didn't mean to upset you, Gabi. I only wanted to catch up after all these years."

"So did I," she admitted honestly, "but it's late and you have to be on duty in the morning."

"Don't leave me yet," he implored. His compelling mouth was too close to hers. She felt the warmth from his body as he slid his hands around her and pulled her into him. "It's been too long since we last kissed each other. I have to kiss you again. I *need* to kiss you, if only for old times' sake."

"Jeff!" she cried helplessly as his dark head descended and his mouth covered hers in the old familiar way. Fourteen years might have passed, yet her body seemed to know by instinct where to fit as she melted into him.

But the years had brought changes. He was kissing her with a man's kiss now, hot with desire and an urgency that caused her to forget time and place.

"You always were so beautiful to me," he whispered in a husky voice, slowly devouring her. His mouth roved over her face, kissing, tasting every inch of skin. Eyelids, cheeks, nose and chin...every part of her features knew his touch. Driven by her long hunger for him, she kissed his rugged face, finding the cleft in his chin before seeking the mouth that had set her on fire.

Somehow they ended up entwined on the couch. One of his hands found its way to her hair. She felt his fingers tug gently at her curls, just the way they used to do. Memories surfaced, so sweet and piercing, that she groaned from the exquisite pain of them, and a few tears escaped.

"What's wrong?" he whispered, leaning over her. He wiped the moisture from her temple with his thumb. "I tasted those salty tears."

Her body quivered. "I'm so full of emotions right now, I feel like I'm going to explode."

His lips twitched. "Well, we can't have that. What would Nicky say?"

In her emotional hysteria, Gabi giggled, just as her daughter would have done.

"What do you say we lie here for the rest of the night and just hold each other? For old times' sake."

This was a moment for honesty. "I need you to hold me so I'll believe we really met up with each other again."

He stole a kiss from her parted lips before pulling her against him so her face was buried in his neck. "Do you know how many times I would have killed to spend a night with you like this?" he whispered into her hair. His hand slid up to the back of her neck and caressed her there.

She could only admire his control because she didn't have any. "I don't want to think about the old days. It's too painful."

"Then we won't. We'll concentrate on the present and make the most of the time you're here."

The time I'm here.

Those words reverberated in her head. The walk down memory lane was all he was offering. Nothing more. What could she expect, when she sensed he might not be over his feelings for his ex-wife? Had she been the one to reject him? Gabi couldn't imagine it.

Maybe it was a case of them not being able to live together, or without each other. Whatever had happened, some inner demon had kept him single since his divorce.

Grab tonight, Gabi. It would be the only night without Ashley. Gabi would take this gift and stay in his arms until the sun came up. "I won't move if you won't."

"I'm not going anywhere unless there's an emergency."

"That's good." Knowing in her heart he would keep her safe from anything and anyone, she nestled closer. "I have so many questions, I don't know where to start. What movies were you in?"

He named several dozen titles.

"I've seen at least half of them! I can't believe I was watching you and didn't know it."

His lips grazed her ear. "Every time a film came out, I wondered if you'd see it."

"When I get back to Rosemead, I'm going to rent all of them." His soft chuckle curled through her body like a warm electric current. "What's that work really like?" she asked.

"I can tell you it's not glamorous. Sometimes the days last fourteen hours or more, in uncomfortable situations."

"Like what, for example?"

"Having to stay submerged in water. Some locations are on mountains in a snowstorm, or out in the desert."

"Did you make a good living?"

"In time I drew a six-figure income."

"The way you put your life in danger, it ought to have been a lot more!"

His mouth roved over her cheek and neck, sending

thrilling sensations through her body. "You should have been my press agent."

"Did you have one?"

"Oh, yes. Arnie Freeman."

"I've heard of him."

"He's a pain, but he's good. I needed him to negotiate contracts for me because I was in school and had to balance my time in both places."

Gabi cupped the side of Jeff's face. "What were the most dangerous stunts you ever did?"

He kissed her palm. "The pyrotechnic scenes. It takes hours to set up the charges for a scene with explosions. Most stunts involving motorcycles require careful measurements and the construction of ramps and crash barriers. All my scenes had to be rehearsed as closely as possible to the actual stunt, without any of the risk factors."

She groaned. "It sounds so hard."

"What was hard was having to film stunts multiple times to catch additional camera angles, or because something wasn't right the first time through. But it isn't practical to reshoot the scene. If the chase culminates with an explosion and a motorcycle crash, doing it over becomes too expensive. That's why the film crew wants to be sure the shot is captured right the first time, to avoid costly and dangerous second takes."

"You were lucky to get out of the business before you got permanently injured."

"That was the idea. I'd made some sound investments and was ready to move on to what I really wanted to do. As you know, a person doesn't become a park ranger to make money."

"Neither does a schoolteacher, but like you, I love my work. Ashley goes to school with me and we eat lunch together and go home together. It's been a perfect solution for us."

"She's a perfect little girl."

"I think so, but I'm so frightened now that Ryan's back." She burrowed instinctively against Jeff. He wrapped his arms tighter around her.

"Do you trust your attorney?" She nodded. "Then let him worry about it. You're on vacation with Ashley. With you here, I feel like I'm on one, too. We'll make the most of it. What do you say?"

"You're a very special person," she whispered against his throat. Full of emotion, she felt tears trickling from the corners of her eyes.

"You're crying. How come?"

"Because I know this contentment can't last. Just keep holding me."

"I have no plans to let you go."

At those comforting words, she gave in to her emotional exhaustion and let oblivion claim her.

The next time she became aware of her surroundings, the sun was streaming in the living-room windows and she was alone on the couch. No Sergei. Jeff had thrown a light blanket over her. Was it nine already?

She rolled off the couch and got to her feet. He'd made her feel so secure, she'd fallen into a deep sleep and hadn't heard him leave. What if Rachel had called because Ashley wanted to talk to her?

Before she did anything else, Gabi hurried into the kitchen with her cell phone to find the numbers Jeff had written down for her. Next to the pad, he'd left her a note, with a key lying on top.

"Hey, Gabs—" his old nickname for her almost tripled her heartbeat "—good morning! I don't know about you, but I got the best sleep I've had in ages. Sergei and I will be out checking different campsites for damage since the flood. If you want to go anyplace, take the Volvo. It's full of gas. Enjoy your day. I'll call you later. We'll have dinner tonight at the Ahwahnee. You and Ashley will love it."

Euphoria caused Gabi to squeeze the note in her hand before phoning the Rossiter house. Rachel answered on the third ring. "Hi, Gabi!"

"Hi! I'm sorry I'm calling so late. I can't believe how long I slept in. I never do this! How's Ashley?"

"The children had the time of their lives last night. This morning at breakfast they made their plans for the day, then ran over to Annie's to play horseshoes."

"You've been marvelous to Ashley. I'd like to repay you. How about tomorrow you let me tend Parker, so you get can out for the day and do whatever you want? I'll watch the children, too. I know what it's like to be with your baby day and night. You need a break."

"Thank you, Gabi. I might take you up on that for part of the day. Just so you know, Chase is going to take the kids horseback riding this afternoon. He says you're welcome to join them."

"That's very nice of him. I've never been. Neither has Ashley."

"Then you're in for a real treat. Chase is an expert horseman. He's been teaching them how to ride. It's one of their favorite things to do. They've been on a lot of trails into the high country."

"What lucky children. Tell me how to find Annie's house and I'll go over there as soon as I've gotten dressed."

Once she'd been given directions, Gabi hung up and headed for the bathroom. First, of course, she needed to wash her hair and take a shower. Ashley would need one, too, and a change of clothes.

Gabi wished she had a new outfit to wear for Jeff tonight. Being with him again made her excited to be alive in a brand-new way. She couldn't wait until he got home from work. In fact, the more she thought about it, the more she wanted to go over to headquarters and visit him instead of going riding. Take him a sack lunch. That is, if Ashley was willing to go riding without her.

It wasn't until she was drying her hair that it struck Gabi she'd fallen into the old pattern of waiting for him. Fourteen years later and Jeff was still at the center of her universe. She'd marked time by him before, and was doing it again.

What was she doing, thinking she could stay here until school started? Was she out of her mind?

Yes. She was!

Before she left for the Jarvises' house, she would phone and make reservations for a flight to Los Angeles on Sunday. Though she and Ashley faced possible danger at home, they would face a different kind of pain and suffering when they had to say goodbye to Jeff for good.

Sunday was it. End of vacation in paradise. It *had* to be.

WHILE JEFF WAS ON his cell phone with one of the crew chiefs, Diane poked her head in the door of his office. *"You have a visitor,"* she mouthed.

He nodded and signaled for her to show whoever it was in. When Gabi stepped over the threshold, Jeff almost dropped the phone. She wore a short-sleeved, celery-green blouse with a white wraparound skirt her figure did wonders for.

He clicked off and got to his feet. "Come on in and sit down."

"I hope you don't mind my disturbing you. I brought you lunch." She put the sack on his desk before sinking into a chair.

"Thank you. No one's ever done this for me before." He shut the door for privacy. It was like old times, eating lunch together. They'd never cared what they did as long as they could be within sight of each other.

"You've been so good to Ashley and me, I wanted to reciprocate, even if it's not much."

It was a good thing she'd brought him something to eat. Otherwise he was in danger of pinning her against the wall and kissing the daylights out of her. "Where is she?"

"Chase took her horseback riding with Nicky and Roberta."

"She'll have the time of her life." Jeff inhaled the bacon-and-tomato sandwiches she'd made. They'd always been his favorite. Everything she did was turning him inside out.

Gabi looked around her. "So this is your domain."

"Yup. What do you think?"

"It's kind of messy, like your old bedroom used to be."

Jeff laughed out loud. "You met my secretary, Diane. She's dying to get in here and go to town, but I told her if she touched one thing, I'd fire her."

"Uh-oh." Amusement lit her heavenly blue eyes. "I know you're a busy man. Is there anything I can do for you before I go?"

He could think of several things. "Yes. Enjoy yourself."

She stared into his eyes. "I am."

His pulse raced. "What are you going to do for the rest of the afternoon?"

"Roberta's mother told me to visit the museum. I'm headed there now." Gabi stood up before he was ready to let her go. "No, no. Stay where you are." She started for the door.

"I'll be home by six and we'll go to dinner."

"Ashley's counting the hours."

So was Jeff.

THE FLOOD HAD DONE its share of damage in Yosemite Valley. Jeff had put in some long days making assessments and assigning work crews. Now it was Friday evening and he was off duty until Sunday morning. He couldn't leave headquarters and get home to Gabi and Ashley fast enough.

About an hour ago he'd given her a heads-up that he'd be there by five. Once he'd loaded the motorcycle, they'd be leaving for North Fork. With the benefit going on tomorrow, he wanted to get settled in for a good night's sleep. Early in the morning he'd do a couple of test runs at the arena while no one was around.

When he pulled into the driveway with Sergei, Ashley was sitting on the front porch waiting for him. "Hey, Ash!" he called, using his pet name for her. Living under the same roof felt so natural, as if the three of them had always been together.

There'd been no repeats of the other night, when he'd come close to begging Gabi to go to bed with him so he could make love to her. The fire was there, stronger and hotter than before, almost beyond his control, but the timing was off. With her first court-case date coming up, he needed to be patient until she knew what she was facing. Then he'd speak his mind, and they'd go from there, because he planned for this happiness to continue forever.

The second Ashley saw him, she ran over to the truck, her face wreathed in smiles. "Jeff!" she cried, before launching herself at him, almost knocking his hat off. "I've been waiting and waiting."

Those strong arms flung around his neck—hugging him surprisingly tight—found their way right around his heart. He loved this precious cherub, whom he secretly thought of as his little Gabi.

Sergei made some strange sounds. "I do believe he's jealous of your attention to me." He kissed the top of her head. "Come on. Let's go in the house and find your mom."

"I'm right here," Gabi said from the porch.

Yes, she was. Standing there looking unbelievably beautiful in a cherry-red short-sleeved top and jeans. Though she'd always been modest in her dress, the curves of her body could never be hidden. With her black hair and fair complexion, she looked incredible in any color, but he had to admit he was partial to red on her.

While Ashley played with Sergei for a minute, Jeff climbed the steps. Gabi's flowery scent reached out to him like a living thing. "Any phone calls from Bev?"

"No."

"That's good." He stared into Gabi's eyes. The purple glints were more striking than usual because of her coloring and top. "It appears Ryan has gotten the word from his attorney, and you can relax."

"I am relaxed."

"Not completely. But I've got a weekend planned that's guaranteed to make you forget your worries. All I have to do is load the motorcycle in the back of the truck and we'll be off." Last night he'd packed the gear he'd need, and was ready.

"How can I help?"

"If you want to open the garage door for me, I'll back in. But first I'll change out of my uniform."

He headed for the bedroom and a quick shower. Afterward he put on a gray crewneck and Levi's. Once he'd pulled on his cycling boots, he loaded his cycle in the truck bed using his fully powered ramp. Last of all he stowed their suitcases.

With that accomplished, he locked up the house. Ashley had already climbed in the backseat with Sergei. Jeff helped Gabi into the front. It took all his willpower to keep his hands to himself instead of pulling her into his arms.

After shutting her door, he went around to the

driver's seat and they were off. When he dropped by Chase's house, Gabi darted him a questioning glance.

"They're going to keep Sergei for us until Sunday morning."

"How come?" Ashley piped up from the rear.

"If I wasn't doing a show, we'd take him with us."

"Oh. I'm going to miss you, Sergei."

"He'll miss you more," Jeff replied. He got out and held the door open for the dog.

Roberta came outside and took the end of the leash from him. "I wish we could see you ride your motorcycle, but Dad says someone has to hold down the fort."

Jeff chuckled. "He's right. See you Sunday morning."

"I'll take good care of him."

"Don't I know it!" He tousled her hair before getting back in the truck.

Ashley put her head out the window. "See you later, Roberta."

"Have fun!" The older girl waved as they drove away.

On their way out of the village, Ashley said, "Nicky wanted to come to North Fork with us, but his mom said they had other plans."

Gabi flashed Jeff a telling glance. He could read her mind. They were both aware that Nicky would have a difficult time waiting for Ashley to come back to the park. It was funny and touching at the same time.

"Guess where we're going to have dinner?" Jeff tossed out the question over his shoulder.

"McDonald's?"

"No. Think fish."

"Hmm. I can't guess."

"Crabcakes Restaurant."

"No, we're not," Ashley giggled. "Sponge Bob's not real."

"I'm not talking about the cartoon."

By now Gabi was smiling. She'd thought Jeff had made it up, too. "Tell you what. If I'm right and you're wrong, you both have to give me a present."

"What kind?"

"I'll let you know when the time comes."

Gabi's eyes slid away from him and out at the scenery. She knew what kind of present he was angling for. The sensual tension between them had been escalating since they'd first seen each other in the village parking area.

After lots of songs and stories along the way, they drove into North Fork at seven-thirty. The place was filling up with visitors who'd come to enjoy tomorrow's festivities. Jeff smiled to himself as he rounded the next corner and pulled up in front of the place where they were going to eat.

"What does the sign say, Ash?" He pointed to it.

"Cr-ab-cakes. Hey, there really is a Crabcakes Restaurant, just like in the cartoon!"

Gabi shook her head. "I don't believe it." Her face flushed.

Jeff's pulse raced in anticipation of exacting his reward from her. "They happen to serve excellent seafood. You can get other things to eat, too. Let's go." He helped them out of the truck. "I don't know about you two, but I'm so hungry I could eat a dozen crabbie patties."

Ashley grabbed hold of his hand. "No, you couldn't." But she wasn't sure and looked at her mother. "Could he?"

"Since I was wrong about the name of this place, I'm not saying anything," she teased, provoking laughter from him. The whole evening felt enchanted. He never wanted it to end.

As they walked out of the crowded restaurant a half hour later, he heard a female voice call his name. He turned his head. To his surprise there was Denise, the blonde woman he'd planned to ask out to dinner. He'd forgotten about calling her ever since Gabi had come to the park.

She was standing in line with her date. "Hey, Denise. How are you?" Jeff said.

"I'm good." They both made introductions. "Everyone's looking forward to watching you do your act tomorrow."

He grinned. "I hope they won't be disappointed."

"Oh, please." Her gaze switched to Gabi. "Have you seen him ride?"

She nodded. "Way back when he was a teenager. He left everybody in the dust."

"That I can believe! Well, good luck."

"Thanks, Denise. See you later."

It wasn't too long before Jeff turned the truck into the parking area of the family-owned motel where they'd be staying. It was a good thing he'd made reservations a year ahead, otherwise they'd have been out of luck.

He got the key from the front desk and let them

in their room down on the end. It had two queen-size beds. Anticipating what Gabi was going to say when she realized they would have to share the same room, he turned to Ashley.

"They'll be wheeling a rollaway bed here in a minute. Watch for it while I bring in our stuff from the truck."

"Okay. Can I sleep in it?" she called from the doorway.

"That's up to you and your mom."

SLEEPING UNDER THE SAME roof in three different rooms was one thing. Sleeping together in the same room was another, but Gabi realized there was no help for it. In a week it was as if they'd become a family. She loved it so much, the thought of having to leave Jeff on Sunday was killing her.

One look at her daughter, who'd changed beyond recognition in the past seven days, and she dreaded the goodbye scene, which was going to be a whopper!

Gabi's thoughts flew to Rachel, who'd told her all about Nicky's meltdown when they'd had to leave the park the first time. She'd been forced to consult the child psychiatrist who'd helped Nicky deal with the loss of his parents. The boy had needed help again to get over the separation from Vance when he and Rachel returned to Florida, where they lived. But nothing worked.

In the end, Nicky had hidden from Rachel and Vance so he would never have to leave the park. But it had turned out all right because Vance wanted to marry her and be a father to Nicky.

The same situation didn't exist with Jeff, the perfect

friend and host, who'd kissed and held Gabi the other night for old times' sake, nothing more.

He had deep-seated issues he didn't want to talk about, and preferred his bachelorhood. Clearly, he could have any woman he wanted. The blonde he'd introduced to Gabi outside the restaurant was attracted to him. Gabi had picked up on that immediately. And then there was Ranger Davis, who Nicky said was crazy about Jeff.

Unlike Vance whose first wife had died, Jeff had an ex-wife who still hovered in the background. Only two days ago, while Gabi had been tending Parker Rossiter and the other children, a woman had called Jeff on his house phone and left the message that he was to call Fran. After he got home from work, Gabi told him. He thanked her, but said nothing more before walking through to his bedroom.

Most divorced couples never saw each other again if they didn't have to. Gabi concluded that, for whatever reason, he hadn't been able to let his ex-wife go.

There'd be no storybook ending here for Gabi, who feared Ashley might need professional help when the time came. The fact that her daughter was dealing with the idea of her birth father wanting to be a part of her life complicated her emotions. That was because Jeff was already bigger than life to her. No one knew it or understood it better than Gabi, who'd loved him since her teens.

She was deep in her tortured thoughts when the housekeeping brought in the rollaway, delighting Ashley, who announced she wanted to sleep in it. While Gabi opened it and put it at the foot of the bed against the far wall, Jeff walked in with their bags and his gear.

Ashley watched in fascination as he showed her his equipment. With incredible patience he explained about his black armor-padded leather jacket and pants, the reinforced Kevlar gloves and his shadow-black, high-gloss, full-face Arai DOT helmet.

"Put everything on!" she begged.

"Yeah?"

"Yeah," Gabi answered, hoping he hadn't heard the tremor of excitement in her voice. It had been a long time since she'd seen him in full gear.

Once he obliged, Ashley walked around him, staring up at him. "You don't look like a ranger now!"

"Then how do I look?"

"You're big and scary."

"Does that mean you two aren't going to give me my present now?"

"What do you want?"

"A kiss. I dare you."

Ashley giggled.

With a flick, he raised the shield so she could see his face. His handsome features made Gabi's legs go weak. As for Ashley, she ran into his arms. He lifted her so she could give him a peck on the cheek.

They hugged hard before he put her down.

"It's your turn, Mommy."

"But he's big and scary."

"No, he isn't." Ashley laughed as if the thought was absurd.

No. He wasn't scary, but Gabi was scared, and Jeff knew it. He was loving this.

The hazel eyes impaling hers gleamed mysteriously. Her heart raced as she moved closer to kiss his cheek, but he knew tricks, and trapped her mouth with his. When she would have stepped back, he crushed her in his arms and kissed her to the edge of oblivion, uncaring of their captive audience.

Her heart was thundering so hard, Gabi feared he could feel it through the jacket meant to preserve his life if an accident occurred.

His smile was meant for Ashley. "Now *that* was a present!"

Instead of laughing, her daughter said, "Do you love my mommy?" Her question ricocheted off the walls.

With reluctance, Gabi felt his gloved hands fall away. "What do *you* think?"

"Nicky said his daddy kissed his mommy because he loved her."

"Then there's your answer."

With her eyes glowing like blue stars, Ashley said, "I wish you were my daddy. Nicky wishes you were, too. Then we could *all* live together at the park." She was sounding more like Nicky every day.

Panicked by the direction of the conversation, Gabi opened the suitcases. "You know what, honey? It's time for bed." She pulled out Ashley's Sleeping Beauty pajamas, and a T-shirt and sweatpants for herself. After grabbing the cosmetics bag, she said, "Let's get your teeth brushed."

"Okay."

They gravitated to the bathroom. All the time Jeff had been removing his gear, she'd felt his intense gaze. Ashley had put him on the spot. He had to know something like this would happen by kissing Gabi the way he'd done, as if it was their last day on earth. She was angry with him. He knew how impressionable her daughter was.

By the time they came out of the bathroom, Jeff had gotten in bed and turned on the TV to listen to the ten-o'clock news. Gabi made certain Ashley climbed into the rollaway and said her prayers.

"Good night, honey. See you in the morning."

Ashley kissed her. "Guess what? Nicky's afraid," she whispered.

"Afraid? Of what?"

"That Jeff might marry Ranger Davis."

That Nicky Rossiter had done way too much talking and theorizing. "I'm afraid he worries too much for his own good."

Suddenly the TV went off. Jeff had gotten out of bed and was headed for the bathroom. "What are you two whispering about?"

Heat invaded Gabi's entire body. "Girl talk," she answered, before Ashley could make things worse. "Kind of like your men's talk in Chief Rossiter's kitchen."

"Hey, Ash? Won't you even give me a little hint?"

"We were talking about Ranger Davis."

"Ashley!"

He paused by the bed. "Did you meet her at headquarters?"

"Yes."

"She's a cool ranger, huh?"

"Yes. But Nicky's scared you might marry her."

"It will never happen. You can tell him that for me."

"Oh. Okay."

"Good night. Don't let the bedbugs bite."

"Good night. Don't let the woodpecker peck you."

The bathroom door closed.

Jeff had overheard their supposedly private conversation. He'd brought all the secrets out in the open for a reason, and had to know Ashley hung on to his every word. Gabi only wished she knew what was going through his mind.

When he finally went back to bed she said in a low aside, "You and I need to have a serious private talk, Jeff."

"I couldn't agree more. We could have it now, but I need to concentrate on my performance for tomorrow. Your being here with Ashley makes me want to do my best riding."

"As if you could do anything else."

"That's gratifying to hear."

She swallowed hard. "The benefit you're doing is for an incredibly worthy cause. How did you happen to get involved?"

He slanted her a penetrating glance. "Ranger King's brother was a firefighter. Apparently he and three others were killed in a fire that raged through the forest south of Yosemite. It happened the first year I was transferred to the park. Everyone was devastated and wanted to help the victims' families. I came up with the idea of doing a benefit stunt show."

Gabi's breath caught. "As I've told you before, you're a very remarkable man. Does your father know what you do?"

"Yes, but he's never liked my love of motorcycles, so stays away when I put on a show."

"Sometimes it's hard to be a parent when you love your child so much."

"I wouldn't know," Jeff said in a bleak tone. "After my event is over, we'll find something to keep Ashley busy while we spend the evening talking." He reshaped his pillow. "Have I told you how much I've loved our outing so far? In case you hadn't realized it yet, I'm crazy about your daughter. So's Sergei."

"She loves him."

"All the kids do. Cal and Alex will be back on Sunday night. I'm afraid he's going to see a huge change in his dog. It'll take weeks to get him back to the place where he wants to track bears again."

It would probably take a year before Ashley got to the place where she would stop wanting to be with Jeff. As for Gabi... She couldn't stand to think about it.

"Thank you for being so good to us, Jeff."

"Even if you're upset with me?"

After a slight hesitation, she murmured, "I didn't say that."

"You didn't have to. Remember one thing. You and Ashley are safe with me while you're waiting to hear from Mr. Steel. Monday's court date will be here before we know it. Good night."

"Good night."

Chapter Nine

Gabi drove the truck to the parking area near the open-air, open-ended arena outside North Fork where Jeff was going to perform his forty-five minute show.

She and Ashley walked toward the crowded bleachers set on one side. They'd barely found a spot to sit, at the end of the lowest row, when the master of ceremonies started speaking through a microphone.

"Ladies and gentlemen! Welcome to our annual benefit for the families who've lost firefighters here in Madera County this last year. We're proud and honored to welcome back for the sixth season former Hollywood motorcycle stunt rider and champion Jeffrey Thompson. He's a California hero through and through. You've all seen him in many action films, but didn't know who he was.

"For those tourists here for the first time, you wouldn't be aware he's now the chief ranger of resources and stewardship at Yosemite Park, our neighbor. This death-defying superwonder gives us his best every year to help raise funds for this worthy cause, donating his time, money and talent.

"He'll be roaring in here any minute now to do his

two-hundred foot jump on the skateboard ramp. Following that he'll ride through the ring of fire at the end of the pipe, land on the seesaws, bounce across the pointed blocks and finish up on the ramp. You'll see him do wheelies riding forward and backward while he's perpendicular to the ground. He'll end with his hair-raising rolling burnouts!"

The crowd of at least a thousand broke into thunderous clapping. Besides the staff and mechanics who worked with him, Gabi noticed several fire trucks, police cars and ambulances standing by. The sight prevented her from joining in the applause. What Jeff planned to do *was* death defying.

She shuddered as she looked at the setups. He had to ride in at a certain speed to execute his maneuvers. One error and he could be maimed for life…or worse.

Earlier that morning the three of them had enjoyed the Lions Club pancake breakfast. Afterward they'd wandered around the classic car and bike exhibits. Jeff knew everything about the various models and their histories. He kept Gabi and Ashley fascinated.

From there they moved on to the logging events, followed by lunch and a visit to the Sierra Mono Indian Museum. Jeff left them there while he took off to do a few practice runs at the arena before the show started. Now that the time was here, Gabi had a rock in the pit of her stomach.

"I can hear him coming, Mommy." Ashley couldn't sit still and strained to see Jeff as the whine of his motorcycle drew closer. Suddenly he appeared, shooting like a comet up the skateboard ramp. Gabi's heart plummeted to her toes as he rose high in the air, doing circles before achieving a perfect landing on the descent.

The crowd went crazy, and were on their feet while he rocketed back and forth, doing tricks she didn't know were possible. Ashley stood up on the bleacher to watch, so mesmerized she couldn't speak. Neither could Gabi.

Jeff had always been fearless, but never more so than now. He went through one stunt after another with clockwork precision. Every time he started a new maneuver, a hush went out over the audience, then an explosive crack of cheers sounded as each new challenge was met and expertly overcome.

Running side by side with Gabi's fear was her inexpressible pride in what he'd done with his life, and how his generous, giving nature had been helping so many suffering families over the past five years.

As the show neared the end, Gabi began to relax. Now that he'd done his routine of terrifying aerial stunts, the worst of the danger was over. For the finale he did a series of rolling burnouts that appeared to be one of the biggest crowd pleasers.

He went around in circles, smoking up the place, laying down rubber while his engine screamed. As Ashley put her hands over her ears, Jeff's body was suddenly thrown through the air, causing the crowd to gasp. At first Gabi thought he'd performed one last stunt to thrill the crowd, until she saw all the rescue workers racing toward him.

"Jeff!" she screamed. Grabbing Ashley's hand, she jumped off the end of the bleacher and started running toward the paramedics gathered around him.

"Ladies and gentlemen," the MC said over the loud-speaker, "as you can see, there's been an unfortunate accident. We don't know how badly Mr. Thompson has been hurt. Please stay in the bleachers and out of the way while the medical staff takes over."

Gabi ignored the order and kept moving, but the police had formed a barrier. "Please!" she said, appealing to one of the officers. "I'm here with Jeff. I have to see him!"

"Are you family?"

"No."

"Then I'm sorry."

By now Ashley was crying. "Is he going to die, Mommy?"

"Of course not, honey." She picked her daughter up and hugged her, pressing her head against her shoulder so Ashley couldn't see anything. "He's just had an accident. We have to wait here until he gets up."

Her little body was heaving. "But what if he doesn't?"

"Jeff used to do this for the movies all the time, and he always walked away." Though she hadn't known about his career, it was obvious he'd survived. "He'll do it today, too," she said like a mantra. "You wait and see."

Please, God.

There were too many rescue workers around him to determine what was going on. For Ashley's sake, Gabi was thankful, but the torment of not knowing his condition was killing her.

"At least tell me if he's conscious," she begged the

police officer, who could see she and Ashley were in agony.

"Just a minute, ma'am. Wait here." He disappeared, but came back shortly as sirens blared and she saw one of the ambulances leaving the arena behind a police escort. "All I can tell you is that he's alive and being transported to the Community Regional Medical Center's trauma division in Fresno."

"Thank you."

It was bad. *Stay alive, Jeff. Stay alive, darling.*

She had to go to him. "Come on, honey. They're taking him to the hospital. We'll go back to the motel and pack up, then drive to Fresno and see him."

While she and Ashley hurried to the parking area, she could hear the announcer telling the crowd to remain calm until they had news to report. Gabi supposed she was lucky the police officer had told her where they were taking Jeff. If word got out to the crowd, the hospital would be besieged with calls and visitors.

Once they reached the motel, she threw everything into suitcases, then they left North Fork. En route to Fresno she pulled out her cell phone. Since she didn't have any numbers with her, she called Information to connect her with the park.

When Ranger Davis answered and identified herself, Gabi asked her to get hold of Chief Rossiter and Ranger Jarvis and have them call her back immediately. It was an emergency. She left her number.

Within two minutes Chase phoned, having arranged a conference call with Vance. "What's happened?"

"It's Jeff!" She told them about the accident and

where he was being taken. "Ashley and I are in his truck now, driving to Fresno, and should be there within forty minutes."

"We're on our way and will meet you there." Chase gave her instructions where to go when she reached the city. "It's the best hospital for him. Hang on, Gabi."

That meant they'd be taking a helicopter. Thank heaven. Jeff would need his best friends around. *She* needed them around.

"Do you think Jeff's going to be okay?" The tremor in Ashley's voice broke Gabi's heart.

"Yes, but what we have to do is keep praying he'll be fine."

"Shall we say a prayer right now?"

"Yes, honey. That will help Jeff more than anything."

"Good, because I love him."

So do I. So do I.

Though not a long drive, it felt like an eternity before they pulled into one of the parking lots near the E.R. entrance. No sooner did they walk inside the waiting room than Chase and Vance appeared. They'd obviously come straight from work, because both were dressed in uniform.

For them to fly here meant Jeff had formed deep ties at the park. Seeing them did more to lift Gabi's spirits than anything else could. In a week's time she felt as if they'd all become good friends.

Vance swept Ashley into his arms. She lifted teary eyes to him. "Does Nicky know Jeff got hurt?"

"Everyone knows, and we're all praying for him."

"We prayed in the truck, didn't we, Mommy?"

Her daughter had given such a touching prayer, it would have melted Jeff's heart. "Yes." She looked at Chase. "Have you heard anything yet?"

He shook his head. "They told us it would be a while. For one thing, he's concussed. They'll be doing a CAT scan and other things. Why don't we sit down while we wait? After that drive, combined with what you witnessed, I know you're drained."

"Ashley and I are going to get a drink and a treat," Vance said. "We'll bring back something for you two. What would you like?"

"A cola?"

"That sounds good to me, too," Chase said.

As they walked away, Gabi buried her face in her hands. "It was horrible. The show was almost over. He was doing his last burnout when he went flying."

Chase put an arm around her shoulders. "It's what he used to do for a living. Every so often he rides his bike through the park on patrol. He'll be fine. The good news is he's conscious. You're the one I'm worried about."

She lifted her head. "I'm all right. I just wish Ashley hadn't seen it."

"We can't shield our children from everything. I have some pretty hideous scars on my torso and hip from an accident when I was in the Navy. I used to break out in a cold sweat worrying what Roberta would do if she ever saw them.

"One day when I thought she was gone, and I was shaving at the bathroom sink, she walked in. I thought she'd fall apart, but all she said was, "Do they hurt?" When I told her no, she ran over and hugged me. That was the end of it."

Gabi let out a shaky sigh. "I teach children nine months out of the year and know they are resilient. It's the adults who have a problem. I was so frightened for Jeff, I left North Fork without even thinking about his motorcycle."

"Don't be concerned over that. Vance and I have already talked to the people in charge. By now they've probably hauled his bike to a garage for repairs."

"If there's anything left of it," she whispered in agony, as Ashley approached with Vance.

"Here, Mommy." She handed her the cola and sat down next to her to drink her root beer.

"Thank you, honey." Gabi thanked Vance with her eyes. "This tastes good."

"I'm glad. When you're finished, if you want to go into the E.R. and find out if there's any news, Chase and I will watch Ashley."

She took more swallows of her drink. "I'd like that." She turned to her daughter. "I'll be right back."

"Can't I come and see Jeff?"

"I don't think he's even in there, honey, but maybe one of the doctors will tell me how he is. Would that be okay with you?" Ashley gave a solemn nod. "Will you hold my drink?"

"Yes."

"Thanks." She kissed her cheek before hurrying across the lounge to the double doors.

On the other side, the triage nurse indicated Jeff was still upstairs, but said Gabi could wait in cubicle five. She thanked her and walked around the counter. When she drew the curtain aside, she discovered a striking, thirtyish, dark blonde woman in designer jeans and a blue tank top seated next to the examining table. She was reading a novel.

"Oh!" Gabi blurted quietly. "I didn't realize anyone was in here. The nurse in Reception told me I could wait in the cubicle, but I've obviously come to the wrong one. I'm looking for Jeff Thompson."

By the puffiness around her eyes, it was clear the other woman had been crying. She stared at Gabi for a moment. "No problem. I'm Fran Thompson, Jeff's ex-wife."

Gabi froze in place. "I—I'm Gabi Rafferty, an old friend of his visiting the park with my daughter."

"Were you at the motorcycle event for the benefit?"

"Yes. Ashley and I drove to North Fork for the classic car show and saw the accident."

"So did I."

"I—I wish I could have spared my daughter."

"I don't blame you. It was awful. For years I've warned Jeff he's been dicing with death, but nothing has stopped him."

Was that the reason their marriage hadn't lasted? Because she couldn't stand to see him put himself in constant danger?

"Do you know anything about his condition?"

"I flew in the helicopter with him."

The police wouldn't let Gabi even get near. With the woman's last name being Thompson, she didn't have any trouble staying right beside Jeff.

"I overheard one of the doctors say he could have a broken clavicle, and was definitely concussed, but not severely, thanks to that crash helmet of his."

Gabi stifled her moan.

"Depending on how bad the injury is, they may have to operate. In that case he'll have to stay in the hospital for a few days. He probably will anyway, while they monitor him."

"Of course." Thank heaven there weren't more injuries.

"I always take time off from work to see him ride when he does benefits. My dad's company contributes to the fund. So do I. Jeff will need nursing at the house for a couple of days, so I told him I'd drive him back to the park after they release him."

Gabi's mouth had gone dry. "I—I'm sure he's happy you're here."

"He's done the same for me. When my dad had a minor heart attack last year, I don't know how I would have made it through without Jeff. What I'm hoping is that this accident has put an end to his daredevil days. His work being a park ranger is dangerous enough."

"I can well imagine," Gabi whispered, feeling so much pain she didn't know where to go with it.

"When he got shot a few years ago, I almost had a heart attack before I learned it was a flesh wound to his thigh and didn't kill him."

What?

"He needed help then, I can tell you. While I was at his cabin he fought any assistance, and hobbled around, even refusing to use his crutches. That man has driven me insane more times than I care to remember, but it doesn't change the fact that I'll always love him." The throb in her voice spoke volumes.

"Some men are too independent for their own good."

"You can say that again. Is your husband like that?"

"No, but he has other problems." Gabi didn't bother to correct her on her own marital status, because she couldn't take any more.

"Please excuse me, but I have to return to the lounge, where my daughter's waiting for me. When they bring Jeff down, tell him Ashley and I came to see him and we hope he recovers very soon with no complications."

"I'll do that. What was your name again?"

"Gabi. It was nice meeting you, Fran."

"You, too."

After exiting the cubicle, Gabi rushed outside the E.R. entrance to pull herself together. She needed time to organize her thoughts before she faced Ashley and Jeff's friends.

Last week his ex-wife had left a voice message on his house phone, no doubt letting him know she'd be at the benefit. Evidently she'd been coming to them for the past few years.

Whatever his relationship with Fran, it was clear they were still involved with each other on some level Gabi couldn't figure out. The other woman showed no recognition of Gabi's name. That meant Jeff had never told his wife about her. Until they'd run into each other at the park, Gabi really had been dead to him.

One thing was certain. She was glad she'd met Fran. Her presence in Jeff's life acted like a bucket of freezing-cold water tossed in Gabi's face, reminding her she, too, had unfinished business with her ex, a man who didn't care who he hurt in order to get what he wanted. Tomorrow he was going to court to fight her.

While Fran looked after Jeff and took him home to help him, Gabi was going back to Rosemead to deal with her own crisis. After drawing a fortifying breath, she joined the others in the lounge.

"Mommy!" Ashley cried, and came running. "Is Jeff okay?"

"He's going to be fine, but he might have to have an operation." Gabi spoke to all of them, because she could see the concern in the men's eyes, too. "See this bone right here?" She touched her collarbone. Ashley nodded. "It's probably broken and has to be set. He has a headache, too, but it'll get better with rest. He'll be able to go home in a few days."

"Can't I see him?"

"I'm sorry, but no one is allowed in there right now, so we're driving back to the park. Thank Chase and Vance for taking such good care of us and giving us treats."

Ashley lost the battle with tears. They ran down her cheeks. "Th-thank you," she said in a wobbly voice.

"We'll walk you out and get his suitcase," Chase said in a low aside.

Together the four of them left the E.R. and headed for the truck out in the parking lot. "When we left North Fork, I was in such a hurry, I just threw his clothes in," Gabi said. "I'm sure it's a mess."

"It's a miracle you had the presence of mind to do that much." Chase pulled Jeff's case from the truck bed.

"Drive safely," Vance cautioned her as he helped

Ashley into the front seat and strapped her in. "It'll be dark soon. Call us as soon as you get there, otherwise we won't sleep."

"I promise." Gabi started up the truck, anxious to get away. Jeff's accident had taken its emotional toll on her. Add to that the sight of his ex-wife, who seemed like a nice person, at the bedside, and Gabi was completely devastated.

Ashley was so upset, she rested her head against the window and sobbed, but in time the tears subsided. To Gabi's relief, she finally fell asleep and didn't stir until they'd reached the Yosemite Lodge.

"How come we stopped here?" Ashley had awakened while Gabi was phoning Chase to tell him they'd arrived safely.

"We're going to take our suitcases inside the hotel and leave them. In the morning, we won't have to carry them when we walk over to catch the bus out in front."

"The bus?"

"Yes. It'll take us to the airport in Merced for our flight home."

"I don't want to go home."

"We have to. Remember that Jeff used to be married?"

"Yes?"

"Well, his wife was at the hospital, and she's going to stay with him after he gets out."

"How come?"

"Because she wants to."

"Even if they're not married anymore?"

"Yes. She loves him."

"Oh."

Once Gabi had removed the few items they needed, they approached the front desk and she paid the concierge a fee to hold their bags till morning. The man told her the bus would leave the hotel at 7:30 a.m. That meant they'd need to walk over from Jeff's house by 6:45 a.m.

As soon as they drove to the house, Gabi fixed them each a ham sandwich. With the truck parked in the garage, there was nothing more to be done except put the truck key and Jeff's phone on the counter. Afterward, she set her alarm for six, so they'd have time for breakfast before leaving the house.

They both slept on the pullout bed in the living room. Ashley needed comfort. So did Gabi, who was still dying inside.

JEFF WAS HOPING TO SEE Gabi when he was wheeled into his private room. Instead, Chase and the chief were there to greet him. Not that he wasn't happy to see them, but right now all he wanted was her. Gabi must have phoned them and then decided to go to a motel and put Ashley to bed.

After the orderlies left and the nurse had checked his vital signs, his friends moved to the side of the bed. "We're glad to see you're in one piece," Chase muttered. "Nobody can do the job you do."

"Thanks. To be honest, after my tire blew, I was glad to discover I hadn't lost any of my own parts, if you know what I mean."

"We know exactly what you mean," Vance murmured. "So *that's* what happened. What's the verdict on you?"

"A bruised collarbone and a slight concussion. Much ado about nothing. I can go home in the morning provided nothing new shows up. Where are Gabi and Ashley?"

"She drove them back to your house."

"What?" He tried to get up.

"Take it easy, Jeff," the chief cautioned him. "She was told it could be several days before you were released. At that news, Ashley's heart was on the verge of breaking because she couldn't see you. Gabi thought it best to get her home to bed. She gave us your suitcase so you'd have your things."

Jeff closed his eyes tightly. "I can't believe this happened. To think my cycle flipped right in front of them. Ashley didn't need to see that! It's never happened to me before. There had to be a flaw in the tire."

"Forget it. The nightmare is over and they know you'll be fine."

"I had plans, Chase—"

"You can carry them out tomorrow or the next day. Gabi's not going anyplace."

Vance cocked his head. "The nurse told us your ex-wife had been here. Apparently, she accompanied you in the helicopter. How did that happen?"

Jeff let out a groan. "Our marriage was over years ago, but she still comes to my shows without invitation. She left a voice message last week, asking me to call her back. I didn't, of course. After the crash, I had no idea she'd flown to the hospital with me. All I could think about was Gabi. When they brought me into the E.R., I was so dizzy and full of painkillers, I didn't know what was going on. Later I was told she'd come."

"We think Gabi must have bumped into her when she went into the E.R. to check on you," Vance said. "She was gone a lot longer than I would have expected, now that I realize you weren't in there."

"Oh, hell…"

"It would explain why she left the hospital in such a hurry," Chase theorized.

"I'm beginning to think Gabi could be a lot like Rachel," Vance mused.

"You're reading my mind."

Jeff looked from one to the other. "What do you mean?"

"When Rachel first came to the park with Nicky, she wouldn't give me any indication that she was interested in me because she thought I was still in love with my first wife. I kept waiting for a sign that never came.

"If your ex-wife gave Gabi the impression you're still interested in her, it's possible Gabi might believe she's trespassing on private territory. That's probably the reason she left for the park. How was she to know you're not still hung up on your ex? In her mind it would make perfect sense, especially since you never remarried."

"Did she say anything about talking to Fran?"

"Afraid not," Chase said. "But she was clearly not herself."

Vance's brows furrowed. "I agree."

"I've got to talk to Gabi right now! Damn—she has my phone in her purse. Will you call it?"

"Sure." Chase pulled out his cell and made the

call, then handed it to Jeff. It rang until he got his own voice mail.

"She's not picking up. I'll phone my house. Maybe she's there by now and will hear me." But several more attempts produced no results. He handed the phone back to Chase. "Thanks."

Vance eyed him with a sober gaze. "Ashley was terribly upset over having to leave the hospital without talking to you. You should have seen those blue eyes dripping tears. She's one cute little girl. Nicky hasn't stopped talking about her since Gabi first came to the park. I can see why."

"I love them both," Jeff whispered.

"I've been there," Vance murmured. "She reminded me so much of Nicky when he had to go back to Florida the first time, it was déjà vu all over again. Maybe it's better you can't reach them until morning, after all of you have a good sleep."

Jeff's jaw hardened. "You don't know Gabi. If Fran said anything to upset her…"

A pensive look crossed Vance's face. "Is your ex-wife prone to cause trouble?"

"No, but since the divorce, she's been in denial that our marriage is over. I'm pretty sure she thinks I still care for her because I haven't found anyone else. The problem is, I made the mistake of going to see her when her father went to the hospital for a mild heart attack. He and I were business friends before I started dating Fran. She thought it meant something, and I've regretted that visit ever since."

He watched Vance rub the back of his neck. "Until the very end, my wife's ex-fiancé didn't give up hoping she'd go back to him. Even after she'd said a final good-bye to him, he flew here and checked into the Ahwah-nee, hoping she'd see reason."

Chase nodded. "It got so nasty while we were eating dinner with Nicky, I had to tell him to leave, or else."

Jeff heard what they were saying. "I can't see Fran going that far, but she had to realize Gabi had come to the E.R. for a reason."

"And deliberately scared her off?" Vance said.

"Maybe. It all makes an ugly kind of sense."

"Tell you what. Chase and I are going to sleep in the doctor's lounge down the hall tonight. If Fran shows up in the morning while you're still asleep, we'll be here to let her know—in the nicest way possible—that we'll be taking you back to the park with us in the helicopter.

"If she wants to do anything more for you, we'll tell her the wives have made arrangements to help you out for a few days until you're on your feet. If you're awake, you can tell her whatever you want, but we'll be here for moral support."

No guy ever had better friends. Jeff was humbled by their concern. "Thanks for everything."

"Now you know how I felt when you and the others on the search-and-rescue team helped me pull Annie from that helicopter crash."

Jeff looked at Chase while they both recalled the accident that could have ended his wife's life.

"Get some rest. See you in the morning."

The second they left the room, Jeff rang for the nurse and asked her to hand him the phone. But Gabi must have turned off her cell and there was no answer at the house. *Hell.*

Chapter Ten

Once lunch was over, Jessica and Ashley went into the bedroom of the apartment to play. It gave Gabi a moment to phone Greg. To her relief she got his answering machine and left the message that she was still on vacation and would call him when she got home. But she didn't give him a return date.

After being with Jeff, she knew she couldn't continue to see Greg, not when the feelings weren't there for him. At the right time she would tell him the truth, that she was in love with the same man she'd loved since her teens. But she couldn't deal with anything while her court case was going on.

Gabi looked up at the clock. By now Mr. Steel would have been in court for her show-cause hearing. While she waited for him to phone and tell her what had happened, she checked her messages. There were three calls from Jeff. Unable to stand it any longer, she listened to the first one.

Gabi? Call me back so we can talk. I'm in a private room now. The doctor told me my collarbone is bruised, nothing more. I'll fly home tomorrow with Chase and Vance.

So it wasn't broken! That meant he could have been released from the hospital and flown to Yosemite by now.

They told me you took Ashley back to the park. I won't be able to go to sleep until I hear your voice and know you got home safely. This is the hospital number.

She clutched the phone tightly. What about Fran? Now that Gabi had met her, pictures of the two of them together in Carmel making memories Gabi would never share with him had tortured her during the drive home.

After she deleted the message, the second one played. He'd sent it at 11:30 p.m.

Apparently you've turned off your phone. As soon as you hear this message, please call me—tonight, if you can. I'll give you the number again.

Still no mention of Fran.

After deleting it, she listened for the third one. He'd sent it an hour ago.

The guys flew me home with them. I'm back in my house, Gabi. Why aren't you answering my calls? They think maybe you met my ex-wife at the hospital last night and for some reason were put off by her. Is that true?

Gabi—I didn't ask her to come to the benefit show. Though she'd like it to be otherwise, I've had nothing to do with her since the divorce. Except for visiting her father in the hospital, any time I've seen her after that she's been the one to show up, unwanted and uninvited.

When she phoned last week, I never called her back.

She knew about you before we married. She knew you were the reason our marriage failed.

Hot tears gushed down Gabi's cheeks.

When she realized you were back in my life, she obviously said something that made you run away. I'll never know what was said unless you tell me, because when I was brought back to my room, she wasn't there.

Gabi? I hope you're still listening. I've only ever been truly in love with one woman in my life, and you know very well who she is. Otherwise, why would I have followed you to El Portal and begged you and Ashley to stay with me? Only love would have caused me to fly to L.A. and bring you both home with me.

Heaving sobs of joy shook Gabi's body.

But if your feelings don't run as deep for me, then don't phone me back. Let this be the end. If the love and trust aren't there on your part, so be it. I'm through being crucified by circumstances beyond my control a second time.

"Oh, Jeff…" She sank down on one of the kitchen chairs and listened to the message again, savoring every word. When it came to the end, she saved it and would never delete it.

Almost out of breath with excitement, she decided to look in on the girls before she phoned him back. They were having an intense game of Match-Up. Hopefully, they'd stay engrossed long enough for her to have the most important talk of her life with Jeff.

Gabi went into her bedroom, leaving the door open a crack. But no sooner did she sit on the side of the bed to make her call than the phone rang. She checked the caller ID and clicked on.

"Hello?"

"Mrs. Rafferty? It's Janine, Mr. Steel's paralegal. We're still at the courthouse. Just a moment, please. He wants to talk to you."

Gabi waited until he came on the line. "Mrs. Rafferty?"

"I'm so glad it's you. I've been waiting for your call."

"The hearing just ended. The good news is, you've won!"

"What?" she cried, overjoyed for a second time in the past five minutes. "I'm so happy I can't stand it."

"Your ex decided to withdraw his suit for joint custody of your daughter. He's had a week to consider the stipulation that he must go in for psychological tests and counseling. When the judge asked the attorney if his client was ready to comply, he said Mr. Rafferty refused on the grounds that he'd had counseling in the Army.

"The judge said that counseling had no relevance. The law required him to go through a whole new process because of the gravity of this case, which involved a minor. At that point your ex challenged his opinion.

"It was the wrong thing to do in front of the judge, who told Mr. Durham to advise his client against any more outbursts. But Mr. Rafferty refused to calm down. The judge gave him one more chance to desist, but to no avail, so he declared the case permanently closed. Your ex stormed out of the courtroom. That's the bad news."

Gabi gripped the phone tighter. "Because he'll always be an angry man."

"Yes. I asked that the restraining order still stand until further notice, but my question to you is are you still in a safe place?"

Adrenaline rushed through her veins. "No. I just arrived at my apartment a few hours ago."

"Then leave immediately and stay out of sight until your ex has had a week or so to calm down. Now that the case has been heard and dismissed, he might assume you've come back home, thinking it's safe. My bet is he'll come looking for you and Ashley."

Gabi shuddered.

"Luckily, he has to drive from L.A. to Rosemead, which gives you a little time."

"We're going now. Thank you from the bottom of my heart, Mr. Steel. I'll be in touch with you soon."

Gabi hung up, then jumped off the bed and ran to Ashley's room. "Honey? I've got the most wonderful news in the world!"

Her daughter lifted her head. "Did Jeff call us?"

"Yes. He didn't break his collarbone and he's back home. He said he wants us to come as fast as we can."

"Did his wife leave?"

"Yes, and she won't be back."

Ashley ran over and hugged her so hard she almost knocked her over. Gabi looked at the other little girl. "I'm sorry, Jessica. But we have to leave again. We'll get together soon, I promise. Tell your mommy I'll call her later."

"Okay." She looked as if she was ready to cry.

"Go see her to the door, Ashley."

While they went down the hall, Gabi grabbed her

daughter's overnight bag and repacked the clothes she'd just washed and dried. Then she did her own packing, including their toiletries. There was only one thing left to do. She put on the T-shirt Jeff had bought her, and wore it with a pair of white sailor pants he hadn't seen before.

Without worrying about anything else, she locked the apartment door and they hurried out to the car. Since she had filled up the gas tank after leaving the L.A. airport, they didn't have to stop for anything. Once she'd phoned Jessica's mother and made sure Ashley's friend was home safely, Gabi was able to relax.

"Guess what other good news I have for you?"

"What is it?" Ashley asked.

"You remember that your father wanted to be able to see you, and I told you the judge had to give him permission?"

"Yes?"

"Well, I just received a phone call from my attorney. He said the judge told your father it had been too many years, so he doesn't have permission to see you. Now you don't ever have to worry about that again."

"I'm glad, because I want Jeff to be my daddy."

"I know you do." *I want it, too. More than you'll ever know.*

Much as she wanted to talk to Jeff this very instant, the phone wasn't the way she envisioned declaring her love. By the time they reached Fresno to gas up again, she had a plan in mind she couldn't wait to put into action.

As she got out to fill the tank, she noticed another car pull up on the other side of the pumps. It looked like the same blue Forerunner that had been traveling alongside or behind her since leaving home, but she didn't recognize the driver. As long as it wasn't Ryan, she was thankful.

Of course it wasn't Ryan! She'd left Rosemead too soon for him to be following her. She was just battling nerves.

After getting a hamburger, they headed for Yosemite. Every so often Gabi looked in the rearview mirror and thought she saw the blue car again. It had to be a coincidence that someone else had the same destination in mind and was stopping at the same places.

When she finally reached the line of cars headed for the entrance to the park, relief washed over her. It wouldn't be long before they'd be seeing Jeff. Somehow she had to quell the frantic beating of her heart or she would have an accident before she got there.

The same ranger she'd seen before was on duty. He smiled. "Hello, again."

"We can't seem to stay away from the park."

"That's good to hear. Do you have a reservation for tonight?"

"Yes." Oh, yes. "I learned that lesson last week."

He chuckled. "Enjoy your stay."

"You're not going to ask me any questions?"

"Not this time."

As she drove on through, she glanced in the rearview mirror. There was no blue car in the line behind her that she could see. She'd been spooked for nothing. Still, she was glad to be in Jeff's world, where he would protect them.

Ashley looked around, making excited sounds because it wouldn't be long now. "I can't wait to see Jeff."

Gabi took a deep breath. "I know how you feel. Let's stop at the grocery store and pick up a few treats to help him get better faster." Cinnamon hots for starters.

"I want to get him some Hershey's Kisses."

"Those sound good." The area was thick with tourists. Gabi had to drive around slowly before she spotted a parking place. "At last!"

Once she locked the car, they hurried inside the store to buy their favorite candy and chips. They picked up some drinks, too. The line at the cashier took forever, but eventually they went back to the car with their purchases. Gabi pressed the remote on her key chain.

After Ashley climbed in back, Gabi put the sacks next to her. When she closed the rear door and then opened hers to get behind the wheel, a strange man got into the front passenger seat at the same time.

"Mommy!" Ashley screamed.

Gabi cried out in alarm and started to get back out, but he turned and captured her wrist, preventing movement.

"It's been a long time, Gabi. You've been a hard person to track down." He applied more pressure to her arm without Ashley being able to see. "How about introducing me to our daughter."

"HOW COME YOU'RE NOT HOME in bed?"

Jeff lifted bleary eyes to Cal, who'd just walked into his office with Sergei. His best friend had come back from his honeymoon Sunday night a happy man. It hurt to look at him. Jeff was in such a black place, he was close to not functioning at all.

"The house is a tomb. I couldn't stay there waiting for the call that's never going to come, so I drove over here to catch up on some paperwork."

Cal took the dog off the leash. Sergei wandered around to Jeff and put his head on his leg. The canine had human instincts. "Hey, buddy." Jeff rubbed his fur with his free hand.

"Come on home with me, Jeff."

"I wouldn't do that to you. Your wife's waiting for you."

"I'm not leaving you alone." Cal sat in one of the chairs. "You said Gabi's first court session was today. Why don't you phone her attorney? Maybe he knows something that would explain why she hasn't called you yet."

Jeff shut his eyes. In a way he wished he hadn't spilled his guts last night. When Cal had showed up at the house for his dog, it all came out. The guy knew too much and could see right through Jeff. "I have to face the fact that she's gone because she wants to be gone, court or no court. I won't be hearing from her."

"Humor me. What's her attorney's name?"

"Henry Steel. His office is in L.A." Jeff gave him the address on Sunset. In a minute Cal had phoned Information and was put through to Mr. Steel's answering machine. As he was leaving a message, Jeff heard a voice from the hallway.

"What in blazes are you doing here?"

Jeff opened his eyes to see Mark standing in the doorway. "Are you talking to me or Cal?"

"You!"

"This is where I work."

He frowned. "You're supposed to be taking sick leave. Didn't you know you have a visitor? She's probably waiting in your driveway, and here you are looking like the very devil."

When Jeff's head reared in reaction, it pulled on his collarbone, sending pain shooting through him. "Who are you talking about?" If it was Fran, then he was going to have it out with her once and for all.

"Mrs. Rafferty and her daughter. Who else?"

"She's *here?*" Jeff shoved himself away from his desk and stood up, so fast his head swam for a minute. By now Cal had finished his call.

"Yes. Ranger Ness phoned me as soon as she passed through the South Entrance. We're doing our best to keep an eye on her to protect her from her maniac ex-husband. But it looks like that concussion has made your recall fuzzy."

The blood pounded in Jeff's ears. "How long ago was that?"

"Two hours maybe."

Cal's gaze swerved to Jeff's. "She should have made it to your house long before now. I wonder why she hasn't phoned you yet. Did she have a key to your place?"

"No, but when she didn't find me home, she might have driven over to Rachel's or Annie's, so Ashley would have someone to play with."

"Wouldn't they have called, trying to locate you?"

"I don't know, but I'm going to find out."

"I'll call the chief," Cal offered.

Jeff nodded before phoning Chase.

Within a minute, they discovered no one had seen Gabi.

Mark turned off his phone. "I asked Ranger King to check your driveway. No one's parked there. Maybe Gabi took her daughter to eat at Curry Village or the lodge."

"That's possible, but I can't see her doing that without first telling me she was here."

"I agree," Cal murmured. "Come on, Jeff. Let's go look for her."

Jeff moved toward the door. "We'll check every eating establishment. Maybe her ex caught up to her in one of them."

"I'm thinking the same thing. I'll go back to my office and send out an APB to every ranger, staff member, volunteer and concessionaire to keep an eye out for her and her car."

"Thanks, Mark."

They left headquarters through the rear door and climbed in Cal's vehicle with Sergei. But a thorough sweep of every parking lot, plus all the eating places and tourist venues, produced zero results. No one had seen her or Ashley. Gut-wrenching fear for them had replaced Jeff's debilitating depression.

He looked around. "We haven't been in the grocery store."

"It's possible they stopped there for something."

When they walked inside, Tim, one of the clerks, was at the cash register printing out his tape for the day. He looked up at Jeff, eyeing his sling. "Sorry to hear about your accident. That couldn't have been fun."

"It wasn't." He took a deep breath. "Tim? We're on official business looking for two persons who are missing. This is important." He gave the clerk a description of Gabi and Ashley.

The young man nodded. "Yeah. They were in here about a half hour ago. They bought some candy and drinks. In fact, I heard the little girl mention your name, but didn't realize she meant you. They were in a hurry and acted excited."

Jeff's heart rate accelerated. "Was a man with them?"

"No."

"Thanks, Tim."

When they climbed back in the truck, Jeff's phone rang. He checked the caller ID and clicked on, putting the phone on speaker. "Mr. Steel? Thanks for calling me back so fast."

"This is an emergency. No doubt about it. Mrs. Rafferty's ex-husband lost in court today. The case can't ever be reopened."

Thank God. Jeff's eyes met Cal's.

"He left the courtroom in a rage. I called her and told her what had happened. But even though there's still a restraining order against him, I warned her to leave the apartment for a while until he cools off. I'm sure he's armed."

A giant hand squeezed Jeff's lungs. "Somehow he caught up to her here at the park."

"He threatened to hire a P.I. to find her. I'm thinking he must have had one posted outside her house to follow her movements, and got lucky."

Jeff groaned. "His informant could have helped him

catch up to her somewhere along the highway, and he ended up trailing her right into Yosemite Valley. Thank you for your invaluable help."

"Keep me informed."

Jeff rang off, only to hear Cal relating everything to Mark. When Cal clicked off he said, "The park has been put on full alert. Chase is heading a manhunt as we speak."

"Her ex could have taken them to any campground," Jeff said with a clenched jaw. "It's getting dark. If he's decided to end it all and take her and Ashley with him…"

"Hang on. We'll find them. Given when she was in the grocery store, she hasn't been missing that long. His attempt to get her away from the tourists will send up a red flag to rangers on the lookout."

"We don't know if they're in her car or his," Jeff muttered. As they drove in and out of campgrounds, checking with personnel, his cell rang. It was Mark, so Jeff put it on speakerphone.

"I just got a tip from Jose Martinez, a volunteer over at Half Dome. He just spotted Gabi's car in the trailhead parking lot near the Mist Trail leading to Vernal Falls."

"We're on it."

Cal wheeled the truck around and headed in that direction.

Adrenaline shot through Jeff's body. "Her ex is deeply disturbed, Cal."

"We're closing in on him."

"PUT HER DOWN, RYAN!"

"Not on your life. You want to go hiking with your

daddy, don't you, Ashley? As long as you don't make a sound, everything's going to be all right."

He was a strong man, six foot tall, wearing a turtleneck and camouflage pants. And he was carrying Ashley over his shoulder, forcing Gabi to keep up with him. Her daughter's terror had to be so traumatizing, Gabi couldn't bear it, but she had to if she was going to keep them both safe until she could figure out how to get away from him.

Half Dome, rising five thousand feet from the valley floor, was an awesome sight anytime, but up close in the moonlight it looked forbidding. Ryan's classically handsome profile was even more forbidding. With Gabi's deepest fear having come true, he was a menacing presence.

Before long they were away from other people, not pausing as they followed a trail into the forest. "You know why I didn't want a baby? Because they grow up and leave you. My parents left, my grandmother left. Everyone leaves. *You* left."

"Your wife hasn't left you." Gabi needed to keep him talking.

"I don't have a wife. I made her up because it would sound better in court. *You're* my wife. I want you back."

A shiver raced through Gabi's body. "If that's true, then let's drive home to my apartment in Rosemead and we'll talk about it."

"You've been hiding from me."

She bit her lip so hard it bled. "I've been on vacation."

"Bev wouldn't tell me where you were."

"It isn't a case of wouldn't, Ryan. She didn't know where I was, because we don't keep in close touch anymore. Ashley and I were at the beach and then came here."

He stopped walking and turned to Gabi. His brown eyes looked black in the darkness of the pines. "Alone?"

"Just the two of us." He already knew that because he'd followed her all the way. "Please, let's go back to the car. It's getting too chilly for Ashley. She needs to be in bed."

"Where were you going to sleep tonight?"

"At the Yosemite Lodge."

"How come you weren't in court today?"

His mind was all over the place. "My attorney said it wouldn't be necessary for me to be there for the initial hearing. Please, can't we at least go back to the car to talk? Ashley's shivering."

He didn't move. "She looks like you."

"Ashley has your bone structure."

"How many guys have you slept with since the divorce?"

Don't let him bait you into a reaction. "I haven't. Ashley's been my whole life."

"You loved her more than you loved me, and she hadn't even been born." The accusation in his voice warned her his rage was building.

"She was a part of you, Ryan. Don't you understand that?"

"Then show me how much you love me."

Gabi was so frightened, she couldn't swallow. "I

can't kiss you the way you want me to if you're holding Ashley."

To her surprise, he lowered her to the ground, but kept hold of her hand. In the other hand he held the gun pointed at Gabi. "Come here."

Don't show him you're afraid.

Without looking at Ashley, she moved toward Ryan and put her arms around his neck. "It *has* been a long time," she whispered against his lips. When his mouth covered hers, she stood on tiptoe and kissed him back, to be convincing. He remained rigid, and finally lifted his head. That's when she gave him a powerful whack to the nose, using the palm of her hand.

He staggered backward and the gun went off. She heard her daughter scream, and suddenly half a dozen rangers converged on them, wrestling Ryan to the ground.

"Ashley!" she cried in panic.

"She's right here, safe with me," a deep, familiar male voice said. Gabi spun around to see Ashley crushed in Jeff's arms, hugging him for dear life while she sobbed. Gabi ran to him and was caught up in an embrace that locked the three of them together.

"How did you know we came? How did you find us?" she cried into the side of his neck.

"With a lot of help. Thank heaven we got here in time," he whispered fiercely. He sounded as shaken as they were.

"Ryan's sick. He needs help."

"He'll get it. Come on. My best friend, Cal, is back. He'll drive us home in his truck. After a thorough investigation, Mark will make sure your car gets returned."

When they reached the trailhead, Jeff made the introductions before Cal pulled their suitcases from the car and put them in his truck. Gabi told Jeff to sit in the front seat holding Ashley, who refused to let go of him, while she and Sergei sat in back.

Shudder after shudder attacked Gabi's body as her mind replayed the horrifying events of the past hour. If it wasn't for Jeff, the outcome would have been so different.

He headed her list of heroes, but there were other people to thank for their heroics—Mr. Steel among them. He'd shown the concern of a father, telling her to go to a place of safety. One day soon she'd find a way to thank him and all Jeff's colleagues who'd put their lives on the line for her and Ashley tonight. At any time, one or more of them could have been shot. Once, Jeff had been shot while on duty. She had yet to hear about it from his lips.

During the drive to his house she rested her head against the back of the seat and listened as Cal and Jeff spoke calmly on their cells to the other rangers. They were like a close-knit family, always watching each other's backs while they did the job needing to be done at the moment, whatever it was. Her admiration for their work ethic was off the charts.

Jeff had always been a hard worker, but by becoming a park ranger, he'd found his niche in this noble community of devoted men and women. It was a very rare society. Young as little Nicky Rossiter was, he sensed it was something special. That's why he held Vance in such high esteem. Gabi did, too.

The man in charge of all the others had to be remarkable. Because of the way he organized and ran the park, the rangers had been able to catch up to her and Ashley sooner rather than later, when there could have been devastating consequences. Vance Rossiter went on that list of people Gabi owed. In fact her heart was so full of gratitude, her face was wet with tears by the time they pulled up in Jeff's driveway.

Cal jumped down and helped everyone out. Then he brought up the rear with the suitcases and her purse. After Jeff opened the front door and carried Ashley on through the house, Gabi turned to his friend, wiping tears from her eyes.

"I'll never be able to thank you enough for all you've done. I wish I could do something really spectacular for you in return."

The handsome, dark blond ranger broke into a smile. "You already have." He lowered the bags to the floor.

"What do you mean?"

He eyed her for a long moment. "Jeff and I have been friends for years. I've always known some element was missing in his life, preventing him from being truly happy. When he found out you'd come back to the park today, the look on his face was something I'll never forget. That's the most spectacular thing you could have done for me and everyone else who cares about him."

Moved beyond words, Gabi reached out and gave Cal a hug.

After he left, she locked the door and carried the bags through the house. She found Jeff and Ashley in his bedroom. He was seated on the side of the bed, cradling her in his arms like a baby. The sweet expressions on their faces touched Gabi's heart.

"I told Mommy I wanted you to be my daddy."

"And what did she say?" He kissed the tip of Ashley's nose.

Gabi stepped inside the room and lowered the cases. "That I want you to be my husband as soon as it can be arranged."

Jeff lifted his head. She felt his gaze travel over her oh so slowly, finally stopping at the writing on the T-shirt he'd given her. "When I showed up at Bev's after your birthday, I planned to take you to Las Vegas and marry you that very day."

"I would have gone with you. In fact, I would have married you at seventeen if it had been possible."

Ashley sat up. "Can we all sleep together tonight?"

Without saying a word, Jeff lay back on the pillows and carefully placed Ashley in the middle of the bed. Gabi turned off the light and walked around the other side. She lay down and turned to her daughter, giving her a kiss on the cheek.

"You don't ever have to be afraid again, honey. Your birth father is very sick and has been taken away to a place where he can't get out, but he'll receive all the help he needs."

"I'm not scared. Jeff's going to be my daddy." She snuggled down between them. "Can I tell Nicky tomorrow?"

Gabi reached across and slipped her fingers into Jeff's dark hair. "You can tell the whole world we're going to get married and be a family."

At her words, Jeff lifted his free hand to clasp hers hard.

"But you're supposed to teach school," Ashley said worriedly.

"I'm going to quit my job. For now, all I'm going to do is take care of you and Jeff."

"Goody. Can we get a dog?"

"Tell you what, Ash." Jeff spoke at last, sounding more emotional than she'd ever known him to be. "Day after tomorrow we'll have a party. When Cal comes, you ask him if he knows if there's a dog we can buy."

She sat up again. "You mean like Sergei?"

"If I remember right, he told me his dog has a couple brothers."

"Roberta wants a dog like Sergei, too!" Suddenly, she scrambled off the bed. "I have to go to the bathroom. I'll be right back. Don't go away."

"We're not going anywhere," he murmured.

The second she left the room, Gabi rolled into Jeff, who was waiting for her. "Oh, darling!" she cried, but then his mouth stifled all other sounds. For a few minutes they were engulfed in mindless rapture.

He covered her face with kisses. "I have two more days of sick leave coming. How about we fly to Reno tomorrow and get married? We'll take Ashley with us and come right back. At the party we'll announce we're husband and wife."

"I've wanted that for too long."

Chapter Eleven

Two days later Nicky and Roberta showed up at the front door with Samson, delighting Ashley, who'd been waiting for them. While Gabi fed them toast and jam in the kitchen, her daughter told them all about Jeff's accident. They were keeping the news of their marriage a secret.

After the children had run out of questions about all the stunts Jeff had performed on his motorcycle, they went outside to play. Gabi knew Ashley wouldn't say anything about their wedding.

The only other person who knew was Jeff's father. They'd phoned him after the ceremony and invited him to come and stay with them as soon as he could. The older man had been so choked up with emotion, he could hardly talk as he welcomed Gabi into the family.

When she told him she'd always loved him, he wept for the part he'd played in keeping them apart. Gabi had declared she was so happy nothing else mattered. For that, Jeff gave her a kiss to die for.

With the house quiet now, Gabi took advantage of her freedom and washed her hair. Standing beneath the shower, she relived what had happened last night after Ashley had fallen asleep. Gabi and Jeff must have made love till dawn. Her body throbbed with her need of him. It always would.

She felt sorry for every woman who didn't have a husband and lover like Jeff. Being in his arms meant ecstasy beyond comprehension. When he'd had to leave for work this morning, she'd held on to him, unwilling to let him go, because she needed him so desperately. He'd responded by making love to her again, with such hungry passion she'd felt transformed.

How would she be able to wait until tonight?

After choosing to wear her blue, two-piece cotton suit, she hurried into the kitchen to get the cooking done for the party. She fixed tortilla pie, then made Jeff's mother's potato salad and brownies. As she was putting the dessert and salad in the fridge, she heard the children's happy shouts.

Jeff was home.

He'd left the house at seven to deal with an urgent matter. Her heart thundered in her chest, but she forced herself to walk—not run—through the house to open the front door to her brand-new husband. Since he'd left their bed early this morning, she'd been breathlessly waiting for his return.

"Oh." It was Cal rather than Jeff getting down from his truck. He strode toward her, wearing his uniform, with Sergei trotting alongside him. "Now you look more like the ranger who was in the newspaper with your famous dog."

His mouth quirked in amusement, but then he sobered. "How are you since your horrendous experience the other night?"

"Ashley and I are better than I would have dreamed."

"I'm glad to hear it."

"If Jeff and I have any worry, it's that your dog went to pot—his words, not mine—while you were away. He's afraid you'll never trust him again with Sergei."

Laughter rang in the air. "It looks like your daughter is my new competition."

"She took him on a lot of walks, with Nicky and Roberta."

"He would have loved that. Jeff told me you and Ashley arrived at Yosemite on the day of my wedding."

"Yes. He said it was the most magical ceremony he'd ever seen."

"It was."

"Belated congratulations." She gave him a big hug. "Thank you again for coming to our rescue the other night. I was so afraid Ashley might get hurt, or...or killed."

"Jeff was in agony. None of us would have wanted to be around him if anything had happened to you or your daughter."

Suddenly the children crowded round, with Nicky squeezing in the middle. "How was your honeymoon?"

Trust him to ask. Cal smiled down at him. "I bet it was as good as yours. Who's your new friend? I saw her the other night, but I don't think she remembers me."

"This is Ashley Rafferty from Rosemead. She's almost eight and will be going into second grade. She's pretty good at Match-Up and Sergei likes her."

Gabi could see Cal's shoulders were shaking from laughter. "How are you today, Ashley?"

"Good. I love your dog."

"I can tell Sergei loves you, too."

Gabi saw her daughter give him a sweet smile. "Jeff let him sleep on my bed."

"Has he chased any bears away lately?"

"No. We haven't seen *one*. I wish I had a dog like him."

"That's what Jeff told me."

"Where is Jeff, Mommy?" The million-dollar question for Ashley.

"At work, but he'll be home soon."

"I hope so!" she cried, before running back across the lawn with her friends.

Cal followed Gabi into the kitchen. "It smells fantastic in here. What can I do to help?"

"Not a thing."

"Then I'll run home and bring Alex back. I've been hard at work and I'm starving."

"I'm glad. I made enough food for an army."

"You need to when Jeff is hungry, but you would already know that since you're an old friend," he teased. "We'll be right back." Then he was gone.

Heat swamped Gabi's cheeks. Had Jeff already told him they were married? Cal was his best friend, after all.

Five minutes later he returned with his stunning blonde wife, and introduced them before he disappeared into the other room.

"That was a wonderful picture of you in the newspaper, Alex. I'm impressed you headed such a worthy project," Gabi said.

"Thank you. Those teens are the greatest. They all want to come again next summer."

"I can see why. It's paradise here." They chatted for a few more minutes while Gabi finished preparing the food. Alex pitched in to help put everything out on the dining-room table.

"How long will you be at the park?" she asked.

"I— I'm not certain," Gabi replied. If Jeff didn't get home soon, she was going to burst from having to keep their secret.

"Cal told me you've been through a horrendous ordeal with your ex-husband. I can't imagine how frightening it would have been to have a gun pointed at you. Cal saw everything. They were just about to take your ex-husband down when he said you did a self-defense move on him that rivaled James Bond."

"Hardly." Gabi's voice shook. "It's amazing what you'll do for your child."

"I have yet to find out what it's like to have a baby, but we're trying for one."

"How exciting!" Just as she spoke, they both heard noises coming from outside. It seemed as if pandemonium had broken out. "What on earth?"

Alex hurried through the house with her and onto the front porch. Everyone had arrived for the party— husbands, wives, kids, dogs. But Gabi only had eyes for her husband, who she discovered in the bed of his truck with Chase.

Suddenly they jumped down, followed by two dogs that looked almost identical to Sergei. Jeff walked over to Ashley, whose eyes were round with surprise. He knelt by her.

"Meet your new dog, Ash. He's very adventurous and his name is Yuri. He's Sergei's brother."

Ashley hugged the dog as if she'd known him forever. Jeff handed her the leash. "Go on and take him for a walk, but hold on tight. You have to show him who's in charge."

She giggled and started running around with him.

By now Chase had hunkered down in front of Roberta, who was so happy, she was close to choking on her tears. The dog's fur was getting all wet. "This is Peter, sweetheart. He's the other brother of Sergei and Yuri. The breeder in Redding told me he has a gentle nature and will be perfect for you."

The childrens' shouts of joy could be heard throughout the valley. For the next few minutes it was a virtual dog lovefest, with Nicky and Samson getting in the mix.

If Gabi had thought there wasn't anything more she could love about Jeff, she was wrong. His capacity for giving was endless. In front of everyone, she moved toward him, unable to hold back her emotions any longer.

Jeff saw her coming and stood up. When she reached him, he put his hands on her shoulders, turned her around and drew her close. "If I could have everyone's attention for a minute."

Eventually quiet reigned.

He tugged her against him, kissing her nape. "Gabi and I want you guys to be the first to know we've been madly in love for fourteen years and finally got married in Reno yesterday. Ashley was our witness."

Amid the cheers and ecstatic congratulations, Gabi's daughter walked her new dog over to stand by them, her face beaming. "He's my daddy now."

Nicky raced across to the grass to Jeff. "Dad said it was about time."

"Nicky!" his parents cried in exasperation.

Jeff looked down at Gabi, his hazel eyes burning with desire. "Your dad's right, Nicky. That's why he's the chief."

So saying, he pulled the love of his life into his arms.

* * * * *

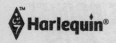

REQUEST YOUR FREE BOOKS!
2 FREE NOVELS PLUS 2 FREE GIFTS!

◊ Harlequin·

American ★ Romance®

LOVE, HOME & HAPPINESS

HARI1B

New York Times *and* USA TODAY *bestselling author*
Maya Banks presents a brand-new miniseries

PREGNANCY & PASSION

When four irresistible tycoons face
the consequences of temptation.

Book 1—ENTICED BY HIS FORGOTTEN LOVER

Available September 2011 from Harlequin® Desire®!

Rafael de Luca had been in bad situations before. A crowded ballroom could never make him sweat.

These people would never know that he had no memory of any of them.

He surveyed the party with grim tolerance, searching for the source of his unease.

At first his gaze flickered past her, but he yanked his attention back to a woman across the room. Her stare bored holes through him. Unflinching and steady, even when his eyes locked with hers.

Petite, even in heels, she had a creamy olive complexion. A wealth of inky-black curls cascaded over her shoulders and her eyes were equally dark.

She looked at him as if she'd already judged him and found him lacking. He'd never seen her before in his life. Or had he?

He cursed the gaping hole in his memory. He'd been diagnosed with selective amnesia after his accident four months ago. Which seemed like complete and utter bull. No one got amnesia except hysterical women in bad soap operas.

With a smile, he disengaged himself from the group

around him and made his way to the mystery woman.

She wasn't coy. She stared straight at him as he approached, her chin thrust upward in defiance.

"Excuse me, but have we met?" he asked in his smoothest voice.

His gaze moved over the generous swell of her breasts pushed up by the empire waist of her black cocktail dress.

When he glanced back up at her face, he saw fury in her eyes.

"Have we *met?*" Her voice was barely a whisper, but he felt each word like the crack of a whip.

Before he could process her response, she nailed him with a right hook. He stumbled back, holding his nose.

One of his guards stepped between Rafe and the woman, accidentally sending her to one knee. Her hand flew to the folds of her dress.

It was then, as she cupped her belly, that the realization hit him. She was pregnant.

Her eyes flashing, she turned and ran down the marble hallway.

Rafael ran after her. He burst from the hotel lobby, and saw two shoes sparkling in the moonlight, twinkling at him.

He blew out his breath in frustration and then shoved the pair of sparkly, ultrafeminine heels at his head of security.

"Find the woman who wore these shoes."

Will Rafael find his mystery woman?
Find out in Maya Banks's passionate new novel
ENTICED BY HIS FORGOTTEN LOVER
Available September 2011 from Harlequin® Desire®!

Love Inspired

Everything Montana Brown *thought* she knew about love and marriage goes awry when her parents split up. Shaken, she heads to Mule Hollow, Texas, to take a chance on an old dream—being a cowgirl…while trying to resist the charms of a too-handsome cowboy. A wife isn't on rancher Luke Holden's wish list. But the Mule Hollow matchmakers are fixin' to lasso Luke and Montana together—with a little faith and love.

Her Rodeo Cowboy
by Debra Clopton

MULE HOLLOW
HOMECOMING

Available September wherever books are sold.

www.LoveInspiredBooks.com

LI87691

Harlequin®

ROMANTIC
SUSPENSE

NEW YORK TIMES BESTSELLING AUTHOR

RACHEL LEE

The Rescue Pilot

Time is running out...

Desperate to help her ailing sister, Rory is determined
to get Cait the necessary treatment to help her fight
a devastating disease. A cross-country trip turns into
a fight for survival in more ways than one when their plane
encounters trouble. Can Rory trust pilot Chase Dakota
with their lives, and possibly her heart?

**Look for this heart-stopping romance in September
from *New York Times* bestselling author Rachel Lee
and Harlequin Romantic Suspense!**

Conard County THE NEXT GENERATION

Available in September wherever books are sold!

www.Harlequin.com.

RSRL27741